Whisker and Whispers

Where Every Clue Begins with a Cat

Tumblebrook Mysteries
Book 5

Ellen Le Teace

Bradford Press

Chapter 1

The Festival Begins

It was the kind of morning that only arrived once a year in Tumblebrook—the kind that made people believe in fresh starts and blooming things. The sun rose over the small Minnesota town with painterly grace, casting golden rays across shingled rooftops, dew-laced gardens, and the winding path leading to the Tumblebrook Inn. Birds chirped in perfect harmony, flower petals unfolded like applause, and the air smelled of lilac, lemon balm, and freshly cut grass.

Amelia Farnsworth stood on the wide front steps of her inn, clipboard in hand, her hair pinned back with more hope than hairspray, and an apron dusted with flour and speckled with soil. Around her, volunteers bustled about with folding chairs and bunting, while the scent of warm scones drifted from the open kitchen window.

Today marked the beginning of the Garden Festival—Tumblebrook's most cherished annual tradition.

For Amelia, it was more than a celebration. It was a declaration: that winter had ended, that small towns still held magic, and that flowers really could bring people together. The inn would be at full capacity, the town square would pulse with energy, and if all went well, she'd get through the weekend without anyone mistaking the compost sculpture for modern art again.

She smiled as she surveyed the lawn. Everything looked just right—the striped tents flapping gently in the breeze, hedges trimmed into tidy labyrinths, and rows of lemonade jars chilling in buckets of ice. Even the bees, she noted fondly, seemed to hum in harmony with the quartet tuning their instruments beside the koi pond.

"Is this where the begonias go?" asked a young man teetering under the weight of a flower tray. He glanced at the labeled signs with the unease of someone holding a live explosive.

Amelia stepped down to meet him. "Yes, just beneath the arch. Partial sun. And don't let them mix with the zinnias—they're dramatic."

He blinked. She smiled. "That was a joke. Mostly."

From the corner of her eye, she spotted a stranger lingering near the trellis—tall, too polished for gardening, and scribbling in a leather notebook. She made a mental note to ask Clara about him later.

Before she could approach, Lady Grey—Amelia's dignified and occasionally dramatic British Shorthair—strolled across the lawn like she owned every blade of grass. Which, in many ways, she did. Her silvery fur gleamed in the morning sun, and a pink silk bow adorned her neck—Amelia's latest attempt at feline fashion.

"Oh no, here comes royalty," someone murmured affectionately.

Guests turned to admire her. Children giggled. Tourists fumbled for cameras. Lady Grey leapt onto a bench draped in dahlias and reclined like a seasoned model.

"She knows when the spotlight's on her," Amelia murmured.

"If she had opposable thumbs, she'd run for mayor," came Clara's voice from behind. Clara Henderson—part-time cook, part-time bookshop clerk, full-time bringer of logic—stepped up with a tray of mini quiches.

Amelia grinned. "I see you won the battle with the oven."

"Barely. I had to threaten it with retirement. Want one? Basil crust."

They stood side by side, surveying the flurry of guests. Clara's eyes flicked over the crowd, assessing traffic flow and overloaded centerpieces.

"You know," she said, watching a child attempt to ride a wheelbarrow, "this may be the most chaos I've seen contained within topiary boundaries."

"And we're just getting started," Amelia replied.

By midmorning, the festival thrived. Vendors sold wildflower bouquets and hand-painted watering cans. A face painter transformed toddlers into bees and butterflies. Music floated from the gazebo as a quartet played cheerful tunes. Elderly couples relaxed under parasols, nibbling scones and trading gossip. The scent of honeysuckle mingled with tangy lemonade and the ever-present promise of sunburn.

Lady Grey had become something of a celebrity. She'd moved from bench to arbor and now posed beside a floral sculpture shaped like a peacock while an amateur artist sketched her.

Amelia floated through the crowd like a hostess at a royal banquet. She answered questions about soil pH, pointed out heirloom lilacs, and reassured several guests that the suspiciously lifelike garden gnome by the fountain was not an actor in disguise.

Behind the competition tent, she spotted Doris Finch—café owner and professional gossip—waving gardening gloves like flags.

"They say I used artificial compost!" Doris huffed. "Synthetic! Me! Do I look like someone who fakes her fertilizer?"

Amelia chuckled. "No one with that much dirt under her nails could be anything but authentic."

"Exactly!"

They shared a laugh, and Amelia was just turning to go when she noticed Lady Grey slipping behind the rose trellis. A breeze lifted the bunting. Somewhere, laughter rang out—but the air suddenly felt thinner.

Then came the mayor's speech. Tom Keegan stood proudly on the gazebo platform, gesturing with the drama of a community theater veteran as he thanked everyone from the garden committee to the high school jazz band. Amelia clapped, though her eyes kept drifting toward the arbor.

She hardly noticed when a guest tripped over a hose—until she was helping them up, laughing politely. When she looked back, Lady Grey was gone.

She walked to the arbor, still smiling. Not panicked.

"Lady Grey?" she called softly.

No response.

Behind the arbor, a narrow path curved toward the older plots. Amelia followed, expecting to find her cat lounging in the sun.

Nothing.

She checked under tables, behind booths, beneath tents. She circled the garden three times before worry truly bloomed.

"Clara," she said, voice low and urgent.

"What's wrong?"

"She's gone. Lady Grey."

They searched—quietly at first, then with growing urgency. Clara questioned vendors. Amelia peered behind hay bales. They whispered her name like a lifeline.

As afternoon waned and shadows lengthened, Amelia's panic edged into her voice. She smiled through conversations, but her hands trembled.

"Where's your lovely cat?" someone asked.

"Just taking a break," Amelia replied, too quickly.

But Lady Grey never took breaks from being admired.

Near the arbor, Clara crouched and picked something from the grass. A tuft of silvery fur.

"This was hers," she said.

Amelia's heart dropped.

"No..."

A gust of wind rustled the bunting. In that moment, Amelia remembered the long, quiet nights after her great-aunt Annie passed

—nights when she might have closed the inn for good, if not for the comforting presence of a purring cat who never left her side.

Lady Grey wasn't just a pet. She was family. History. Home.

By twilight, fairy lights glowed along the hedges and laughter still floated through the garden. But Amelia's world had narrowed to one question:

Where was Lady Grey?

She returned to the bench by the rose arbor and sat heavily, ignoring the petals clinging to her apron. Her eyes scanned the fading light for any flick of a tail.

She whispered, "Please come home."

The festival, once a vibrant bouquet of joy, had wilted into quiet dread.

And somewhere in Tumblebrook, someone had taken more than a cat—they'd taken the heartbeat of the inn.

Chapter 2

The Ransom Leaflet

The scent of cut grass, trampled tulips, and lingering festival popcorn still hung thick in the early morning air as Clara Henderson arrived at the Tumblebrook Inn. Though the sun had risen warm and bright, casting golden rays across the porches and picket fences, the day's cheer couldn't mask the undercurrent of unease curling through the air like smoke. Clara paused at the foot of the inn's front steps and took in the scene.

The inn, with its buttercream siding and prim flower boxes, looked as picturesque as ever. Daffodils nodded in the breeze beneath the windows, and the familiar creak of the front porch swing rocked faintly in rhythm with the morning wind. But to Clara—who'd worked beside Amelia long enough to sense even the slightest shift— the stillness felt wrong. Heavy. Off.

She adjusted the strap of her canvas bag, its weight comforting against her shoulder, and climbed the porch steps. Just as she lifted a hand to knock, the door cracked open.

"You're here," Amelia said, a mix of relief and desperation softening her voice. She looked exhausted, her usual poise gone to the wind. Her auburn hair, typically pinned in a tidy bun, hung in haphazard wisps around her face. Her apron was on backward.

Clara raised an eyebrow. "You're a walking cry for help. Luckily, I brought muffins—and emergency stationery."

Amelia stepped aside with a weary nod, and Clara slipped inside. The familiar scent of lavender polish lingered in the air, but disorder clung to the surroundings: a dish towel draped over the stair rail, an overturned stool near the sitting nook, and—most telling of all—Lady Grey's favorite perch on the windowsill stood empty.

"She didn't come home last night," Amelia said, her voice cracking slightly. "First time in four years."

Clara's eyes narrowed. "Tell me everything."

They sat in the parlor. Morning light filtered through lace curtains, casting soft patterns on the walls. On the walnut coffee table lay a crisp white envelope, unsealed. No stamp, no return address—just blocky print across the front: For the Innkeeper.

Clara pulled a pen from behind her ear, carefully lifted the flap, and withdrew a thick sheet of paper. Six words stared back at her:

If you want her back, stay silent.

She read it once. Then again. "It's not a ransom," she said slowly. "It's a threat."

Amelia hugged her arms. "I found it this morning in a bouquet by the guestbook. I thought Clara Jenkins had sent it. But she swore she didn't."

Clara walked over to inspect the bouquet—a riot of color: foxglove, lilacs, and ivy. Not typical of Jenkins, who favored pink carnations and baby's breath. She examined the base. No card. No florist tag.

"This was placed here deliberately," Clara muttered. "Hidden just long enough to pass unnoticed."

She flipped open her notebook. "Let's build a timeline. When did you last see Lady Grey?"

"Right after the mayor's speech," Amelia said. "I was tying

ribbons for the contest winners. I looked away for a moment to help untangle the festival banner."

"And she was lounging near the arbor?"

"Yes. Near the eastern edge, behind the azalea hedge."

Clara sketched the rough location. "And behind the arbor is the old Vance fence line. Then the forest trail."

Amelia nodded. "Nobody's used that trail in years."

"Unless they wanted to disappear quickly."

Outside, they moved through the side garden, careful not to trample any evidence. The path was scattered with petals and the occasional deflated balloon. As they neared the arbor, Clara slowed. Beneath the sweeping boughs of a cherry tree, she found it—a trail of crushed grass and tiny paw prints stamped in damp soil. Next to them, a faint brown smear.

"She didn't run," Clara murmured. "She followed someone. Willingly."

They tracked the prints until they vanished into underbrush. Clara snapped photos, frowning. Whoever had taken Lady Grey had been prepared.

A breeze stirred the hedge leaves around them. Clara felt a sharp pang in her chest. "She trusted someone," she whispered.

"We can't go to the police yet," Clara added more firmly. "Not without proof."

Amelia grimaced. "You remember the pie fiasco. They turned Mabel's sugar substitution into a federal case."

"Exactly. We'll do our own groundwork first."

Inside, Clara examined the envelope. High-quality paper. Precise fold. Impersonal font. She scrawled in her notebook:

Professional florist? Local delivery? No fingerprints. No tag.

Amelia paced. "Nadine from the garden club might recognize the style."

"Ask her. Quietly." Clara began a to-do list. "Meanwhile, I'll head to Gossamer Fables. I remember something about an old zoning dispute involving your rear lot. Might not be a coincidence."

Amelia stared at her. "You think this is about the inn?"

"I think it's about land. And Lady Grey is the warning shot."

Before they could say more, the front door opened with a gust of wind and cinnamon. Doris Finch bustled in, apron dusted with flour.

"Sorry to barge in," she said breathlessly. "But I heard from Janet at the bakery that Lady Grey's gone. I brought muffins. And I saw something weird this morning."

They blinked at her.

"Out by the trellis," Doris continued. "Near the rose arch where you hung the fairy lights. There were pawprints. Or something like them."

"Show us," Clara said, already heading for the door.

In the back garden, dew sparkled on grass. Clara crouched near the trellis and spotted the indentations immediately. Paw-sized, leading through the mulch. A red-and-gold ribbon fluttered from a thorn branch—tangled, deliberate.

"The same colors from the contest," Clara said. "It was planted."

She pocketed it, noting the slight citrus fragrance. The trail veered through a hedge opening toward the marshy path. Clara hesitated, eyes scanning the thick green silence. A prickle crept up her neck. Someone could be watching.

Back inside, they assembled the evidence on the dining table: the note, the ribbon, the flower samples, Clara's photos.

"This was planned," Clara said. "Someone knows your land. They knew how to manipulate Lady Grey. And they knew the festival would create just enough chaos."

Amelia folded her arms. "And they're watching us now."

That afternoon, Clara made her way to Gossamer Fables. The shop's familiar bell chimed overhead. Mr. Lark, ever the welcoming bibliophile, handed her a mug of rosehip tea without asking.

"In the archives again?" he asked, unlocking the back room.

Clara nodded. "Zoning maps and land records, please."

She spent hours combing through brittle files and faded ink.

Finally, in a file labeled "Parcel Adjacency—Farnsworth 1983," she found it:

Boundary Correction — Pending Dispute.

The lot adjacent to the eastern garden. Registered to the Vance estate. Status: suspended but unresolved.

As she copied the notes, Clara felt the pieces sliding into place. Her gut twisted. Someone had wanted that land for decades—and they were done waiting.

Back at the inn, dusk painted the lake with strokes of rose and violet. Clara sat beside Amelia on the porch, sipping tea. Somewhere beyond the garden, in the woods or marshes, Lady Grey was alive.

Clara glanced at the shadows stretching along the hedge line. "They thought we'd stay silent."

Amelia looked down at her tea. "They don't know us very well."

And Clara made a silent vow: they would not be silenced. Not now. Not ever.

Chapter 3

Petals and Panic

The morning after Lady Grey's disappearance dawned bright and unforgiving. Sunlight streamed through the lace curtains of the Tumblebrook Inn, casting delicate floral patterns across the pine floorboards of the kitchen. The inn—normally humming with the scents of rising dough and fresh mint tea—felt disconcertingly still. Not just quiet, but as if holding its breath.

Amelia Farnsworth stood by the counter, fingers curled around a mug of lukewarm coffee she hadn't tasted. Her auburn hair was twisted into a messy knot, and faint shadows clung beneath her green eyes. She hadn't slept—at least, not in any way that counted. She'd spent the night retracing her steps, whispering into corners, watching windows for the glint of silver fur.

Everything she did that morning—measuring sugar for muffins, refolding dish towels, lighting warming candles under the breakfast trays—was performed with mechanical precision. Without Lady Grey curled on her favorite windowsill or winding between her legs, the kitchen felt unanchored.

Even the inn's familiar creaks seemed uncertain. Outside, the birdsong had softened to an uneasy murmur, as though nature itself sensed something was amiss.

Clara Henderson entered through the side door, sleeves rolled up, a tray of rhubarb muffins balanced in one hand. Her expression was tight, the usual sharpness in her gaze edged with worry. "Anything?"

Amelia shook her head. "Not a sound. Not a shadow."

Clara set down the tray with more force than necessary. "I went to Gossamer Fables. Mr. Lark said she was still by the arbor during the mayor's speech. But afterward—nothing. No one remembers seeing her slip away."

Amelia turned, clutching her mug. "She's never disappeared overnight. Never. She craves attention."

Clara folded her arms. "This feels deliberate."

A beat.

"You think someone took her?" Amelia whispered.

"I think we're meant to believe that."

Before either could speak again, Doris Finch appeared in the doorway, her sunhat slightly askew and apron dusted with flour. "Morning, loves. I brought cranberry scones—and news."

They both turned to her.

Doris dropped her voice. "Janet from the bakery swears she saw someone poking around the rose arbor this morning. Said they were crouching low—like they'd dropped something. Or were hiding it."

Clara straightened. "Where, exactly?"

"Left side of the arbor. Near the azaleas."

They were out the door within seconds.

The garden glowed with color and movement, the second day of the festival in full swing. Tents flapped in the breeze, and laughter rippled through the warm spring air. But in the quiet behind the arbor, beneath the sweeping limbs of the cherry tree, the world changed.

There, half-buried in the soft earth, was a pale ribbon. Clara knelt beside it.

"It's hers," Amelia breathed. "The bow from her collar."

The silk was creased and smudged, the faint scent of rosewater still clinging to the threads. Tiny tooth marks dotted one edge.

"She was here."

Clara scanned the area. A trail of faint paw prints led from the arbor into the underbrush. The grass was flattened where something —or someone—had passed.

"She didn't run," Clara murmured. "She followed."

"Or was coaxed."

They exchanged a glance.

"We need to document this," Clara said, pulling her phone from her coat pocket.

Back at the inn, Amelia's hands trembled as she unpacked the morning flower deliveries. One arrangement stood out—a tall ceramic watering can bursting with lilies and bluebells. Elegant. Too elegant.

No florist tag.

Tucked just beneath a spray of bluebells was an envelope.

Amelia's breath caught. "Clara."

They stepped into the side hallway. Clara took the envelope and opened it with deliberate care. Inside was a single sheet of cream stationery. Six words, typed in a clean serif font:

If you want her back, stay silent.

Amelia swayed.

"There's no demand," Clara said, scanning the note. "No money. No instructions. Just... silence."

"Who would do this?" Amelia whispered.

"Someone who wants control," Clara said. "They picked Lady Grey for a reason."

"She's just a cat."

"No. She's your cat. Your mascot. Your heart. They're using her to unnerve you."

They studied the note. The paper was thick. The typeface, precise. No handwriting. No fingerprints.

"This was planned," Clara said. "They knew your habits. Your timing."

"We can't go to the police. Not yet."

"Agreed. If the sender's watching, any reaction could escalate things. We need to be careful."

That afternoon, Amelia performed her hostess duties with robotic efficiency. She poured lemonade, nodded at compliments, and offered vague reassurances about Lady Grey's whereabouts. But inside, she seethed.

Everyone was a suspect.

The couple from Milwaukee who insisted on a garden-view room. The elderly man who kept wandering behind the kitchen. Even Hugo the magician—his sleight of hand now seemed a little too practiced.

A stranger in a tan blazer asked for the guest library. Amelia watched him linger in the hallway, adjust his cufflink, pretend to admire the wainscoting.

She made a note: muddy shoes. Left lace untied.

When dusk settled over the inn, casting golden light across the lavender beds, Amelia walked the herb path alone. The silence felt sacred—and fractured.

That's when she saw it: another note.

Tucked behind a stone frog statue, half-hidden in clover.

The next bloom reveals the truth.

She stared.

"They're taunting me," she whispered.

Clara arrived moments later. They compared the notes—same paper, same font.

"Whoever this is," Clara said, "knows the garden. The rhythms. The history."

"They know me."

"They're playing the long game. Which means we still have time."

Amelia looked toward the inn. Lights glowed in the windows. Festival laughter echoed through the trees. And in that moment, her sorrow solidified into resolve.

"They think I'll stay silent."

Clara nodded. "They don't know us very well."

Chapter 4

Map in the Margins

O
f all the ways Clara Henderson imagined her Sunday morning, forensic analysis under a magnifying lamp hadn't made the list—but then again, neither had a catnapping conspiracy.

The ransom note sat between a pair of tweezers on the counter in the bookshop's back office. Clara leaned closer, careful not to breathe too hard. The creamy stationery was both chilling and wrong—not just the message, but the way it had been delivered, the faint musty scent, and the unusual texture.

She'd seen paper like this before. Not in a chain store. Not even in the fancier stationery aisles downtown. Antique cream paper.

And that meant only one thing: Mr. Lark's rare collection in the attic.

Clara pushed back from the counter and made for the spiral staircase leading to the hidden loft above Gossamer Fables. The attic wasn't part of the customer experience—too drafty, too unstable, and far too dusty. But it held treasures: rolled-up maps, crumbling almanacs, and brittle pages of hand-penned letters from centuries past.

Mr. Lark had once called it his "sanctuary of parchment." Clara called it her second job.

A puff of dust greeted her as she ascended the final step. Sunlight sliced through the dormer windows in golden beams. Old books lined crooked shelves, and a wide oak table stood in the center like an altar to forgotten knowledge. The air smelled of aged paper and lavender sachets—Mr. Lark's best effort at preservation.

She crossed to the flat files along the back wall and opened the third drawer down. Inside lay several preserved map fragments, each mounted to parchment and labeled in Mr. Lark's spidery handwriting. She flipped through until she reached a faded but familiar piece: a 1911 survey map of Tumblebrook Township.

Tilting the ransom note toward the light, she caught the faint shimmer of a butterfly etched into the fibers.

Identical.

Her stomach tightened. Someone had torn this from the 1911 map.

"You don't destroy town history unless you're hiding something... or leaving a trail," she whispered.

She flipped the map over. On the reverse was a penciled note: "Monarch #7 - Property & Land Commission Notes."

Monarch.

The word made her skin prickle. The Monarch Society. A long-defunct organization that once held considerable sway in Tumblebrook. Official records called them philanthropists. The whispers told a different story—secrets, bribes, land manipulation.

And this map had been part of it.

She carefully rolled it up and slid it into a cardboard tube. Then she picked up the note again. The edges had been lightly singed—likely to obscure its origin—but not enough to disguise the paper's pedigree.

Clara exhaled slowly.

This wasn't just a kidnapping. Someone was reviving a ghost.

Downstairs, she passed Mr. Lark near the front counter. He adjusted his glasses and peered over his mug of cinnamon tea.

"Something the matter, Clara?"

"Just following a hunch," she said. "I'll explain later."

He nodded, solemn. "Careful in those archives. They hold more secrets than most books ever tell."

She didn't ask if he meant that metaphorically.

* * *

Back at the inn, Amelia stood near the kitchen's back door, pacing in tight circles. She turned as Clara entered, her expression a knot of hope and dread.

"Tell me you found something."

Clara set the tube and note on the table. "The paper. It's from a rare map in the attic. A Monarch Society map."

Amelia's brows shot up. "The Monarch Society? As in the old secret club for rich eccentrics?"

"As in the people who practically redrew the town boundaries to benefit themselves."

"And now someone's tearing up their documents and sending us threats?"

Clara tapped the edge of the ransom note. "Not just any documents. This map detailed land ownership... along the river. Near your property."

Amelia slowly lowered herself into a chair. "So you're saying this isn't just about Lady Grey?"

"I think she's the lever. You're the target."

They sat in silence. Wind chimes outside played a gentle, mocking tune.

"Then we need to figure out what's so important about that land," Amelia said.

Clara nodded. "And do it quietly. Whoever did this wants us rattled."

"But we're not," Amelia said, her voice sharpening. "We're just getting started."

* * *

That afternoon, Clara returned to Gossamer Fables. Mr. Lark cleared a space in the back room, producing a magnifier and gloves.

"This Monarch map," he said, adjusting the lens, "is one of the more controversial ones. Lots of crossed-out boundaries. Some say it was a proposal. Others say it was proof of land theft."

Clara pointed to a scribbled margin near the river. "What's that say?"

Mr. Lark squinted. "Looks like... 'Holdings reassigned per council order. No disclosure permitted.'"

"Disclosure of what?"

He frowned. "The Monarchs were secretive. Property disputes, inheritance loops, zoning influence—it all went through back channels. If someone's trying to resurrect that history, we may be in for more than a catnap mystery."

They traced the river line to a dotted marking labeled only "HF-3."

"Could be an internal code," Clara murmured.

"Or a holding file. Or hazard flag."

Clara copied the marking and carefully stored the map. Her next stop was the town archives, tucked into the community hall's basement.

She passed rows of file cabinets, boxes stacked shoulder-high. The room smelled of mildew and patience.

At a far table sat Millie Gregson, the town's self-appointed historian. She wore half-moon spectacles and had a thermos of tea perched beside a stack of yellowed newsletters.

"Need something historical, Clara?"

"Yes, actually. Do you know anything about Monarch Society land surveys? Anything labeled HF-3?"

Millie blinked. "HF-3. Haven't heard that in a while. Let me check the restricted files."

Clara perked up. "Restricted?"

"Well, not officially. More like ignored. Too much red tape."

She shuffled off and returned with a box labeled Historical Fragments – Not For Circulation. Inside were council memos, torn blueprints, and wax-sealed letters.

Millie handed her a file. "You didn't get this from me."

Inside was a 1912 council transcript discussing a proposed river diversion for 'scenic enhancement' to attract investors. A parcel listed under HF-3 was marked 'critical to Monarch valuation.'

"Monarch valuation?" Clara murmured.

In the margin, someone had scrawled: "Property leverage – Farnsworth parcel?"

Her pulse spiked.

She held evidence that someone—maybe decades ago—had tried to seize Amelia's land for profit.

And someone today might be trying to finish the job.

Clara returned the files with a nod and headed for the inn.

Lady Grey wasn't just a beloved companion. She was bait.

And Clara wasn't just holding a map—she was holding the fuse.

Chapter 5

Suspicion in Bloom

The midday sun cast a halo over Tumblebrook, gilding cobblestone streets and blooming gardens in warm gold. The annual garden festival bloomed in full splendor—petals and pastries, laughter and lemonade. Yet to Amelia Farnsworth, the town's cheer felt like wallpaper covering a deep crack in the foundation. Lady Grey was still missing, and the absence of her feline companion made every moment feel jagged at the edges.

The Tumblebrook Inn, usually her oasis, now felt like a pressure cooker dressed in lace and floral bunting. The breakfast shift had passed without catastrophe, but the smallest hiccups rattled her—Clara had burned a tray of muffins, and a guest had grown testy over the lack of almond milk. Normally, Amelia would've smoothed it over with a quip and a smile. Today, each inconvenience thudded in her chest like a warning bell.

And everywhere, questions.

"Any sign of Lady Grey?" Mr. Eldridge had asked at least twice, as if she'd misplaced the cat like a pair of reading glasses. Flyers were posted at the front desk and near the lemonade stand, but the young couple from Duluth still whispered over theirs as if it were breaking news. Their stares lingered. Their curiosity felt invasive.

The world felt staged around her, and she moved through it like a reluctant actress.

Then came Vincent Pike.

Amelia found him in the inn's sunroom, admiring the floral centerpiece she had assembled at dawn. He stood with hands clasped behind his back, an image of composure in a beige linen blazer and neatly pressed slacks. The light filtered through the leaded glass, highlighting his smile—a smile that didn't quite warm the room.

"Miss Farnsworth," he said smoothly, "your arrangement of foxglove and lavender is positively transcendent."

Amelia offered a practiced smile. "We try to keep the indoors as lively as the festival grounds."

Vincent turned toward the window, watching the bustle of volunteers arranging folding chairs on the lawn. "You must be feeling the strain—everything happening at once."

A prickle ran down Amelia's neck. "I'm sorry?"

"The festival," he said quickly. "Coordinating events, hosting guests, and still managing to look so calm. It's impressive."

She didn't respond. He turned then, and with a softened tone, added, "And Lady Grey... such a shame. I do hope she turns up soon."

It was the way he said it—deliberate. Controlled. Amelia studied his eyes. They revealed nothing.

"We all miss her," she replied evenly.

"If I can be of any help, do let me know," Vincent said. "I've always considered myself resourceful in tense situations."

The moment he left, the room seemed to exhale.

Clara appeared in the doorway, dusting flour from her hands and watching Vincent's retreating figure with narrowed eyes.

"He gives me the creeps," she said flatly.

Amelia let out a breath. "And he knew about the note."

"He knows too much," Clara muttered. "And he knows it."

They decided to watch him closely. If Vincent Pike was innocent, he was a curious sort of bystander. If he wasn't—he was dangerous.

The air outside was thick with honeysuckle and chatter. Amelia wandered the festival booths with a woven basket in hand, checking on tea deliveries and chatting with local artisans. She paused to speak with Doris Finch at the café booth, who wore a wide-brimmed sunhat and an apron that had already collected a constellation of flour.

"You look like you've seen a ghost—or skipped a night's sleep," Doris said, offering a rhubarb tart.

"I haven't," Amelia said, accepting it with a grateful nod.

"Still no sign of the feline dignitary?"

"No."

Doris clicked her tongue. "You know what they say—cats and secrets always return, usually together."

Amelia offered a hollow smile. "I just hope this secret has an ending."

Doris leaned in conspiratorially. "Keep your eye on the new man. Vincent. He's always where the tension is, like a cat himself."

Amelia blinked. "Why do you say that?"

"He knows too much. And he never blinks long enough to be thinking."

That afternoon, a delivery arrived at the inn. Clara intercepted it —an arrangement of wildflowers, anonymously sent. Lupine, forget-me-nots, and one white lily standing stark and tall among the chaos.

Amelia carefully plucked the lily from the arrangement. Around its stem, a bit of twine held a familiar scrap of parchment. That same stilted serif font:

Still watching. Don't involve the police. She's safe— for now.

They read it in silence.

"That's it," Clara hissed. "We can't keep this to ourselves. It's time to tell someone."

Amelia shook her head, pulse thudding. "We tell the police, and we lose our leverage. Whoever this is—they want us reacting. We can't give them that satisfaction."

"So what's your plan?" Clara asked, fists clenched.

"We follow the trail. And we start with him."

She nodded toward Vincent Pike, who was charming the garden club with tales of floral taxonomy.

By late afternoon, the festival felt like a dreamscape. Children ran through rows of tulips, their laughter a surreal contrast to the tight knot in Amelia's chest. Clara made her rounds with more intention now, noting who lingered near the inn too long. Who seemed to glance at the window twice. Who stepped just a little too softly.

Later, as Amelia knelt in the herb garden trimming basil for the kitchen, the scent of soil and mint grounded her, but not for long. A faint jingle stirred the air. Metal on metal.

A collar.

She froze. Looked around. A gust of wind rustled the lavender. A single sprig trembled, then stilled—as if something unseen had passed through.

Then silence.

She stared long and hard, heart hammering. Nothing moved. No flash of silver fur. No chirrup.

Still—she knew what she'd heard.

From the corner of her eye, she caught sight of Vincent again, speaking animatedly with one of the groundskeepers. Laughing. Smiling. A man with no cat to mourn, no secrets to weigh him down.

But Amelia had secrets now.

So did Tumblebrook.

And Vincent Pike was standing in the middle of them all.

Chapter 6

Gossip and Garden Paths

Tumblebrook was the kind of town where whispers traveled faster than wind off Lake Superior—and Clara Henderson had learned to listen with precision. Growing up amid the soft gossip and seasonal rhythms of the town, she understood how to separate rumor from revelation, chatter from clue. Ever since Lady Grey disappeared, Clara had felt a slow, churning dread rising in her chest—a combination of guilt, worry, and the unshakable sense that something was unfolding just beyond her reach. She'd thrown herself into the search not only to help Amelia, but to prove something to herself: that she could uncover the truth before it vanished like pawprints in fresh snow.

On this clear spring morning, she sat at her usual corner booth in Doris Finch's café, notebook open beside her, waiting for the day's secrets to unfold. The post-breakfast lull was when the stories started to stretch their legs. The kitchen clatter had calmed, the regulars lingered over second cups, and Doris held court behind the counter, issuing refills and commentary with equal gusto. Clara stirred her coffee slowly, a second spoonful of sugar dissolving as she listened.

Outsiders filled the town for the garden festival, and their voices mixed with the locals' like wildflowers in a groomed bed. It made filtering through the noise more challenging—but not impossible. Clara watched for patterns: lowered voices, furrowed brows, the subtle weight behind a casual phrase.

Two women sat a few tables away, their conversation hushed and urgent.

"I swear I saw someone sneaking through the maze," the first woman said, glancing over her shoulder.

"Probably a teenager," replied the other.

"No, not a kid. Tall man. Dark coat. Slipped in through the east hedge after the concert. Gave me the creeps."

Clara stiffened. That was the night Lady Grey vanished.

She made a quick note: east hedge, 10 p.m., tall man, dark coat.

By the time she looked up, the women were gone. Clara slipped out the back, her mind churning. This wasn't idle gossip. This was the first real lead.

Back at the inn, she found Amelia stacking brochures at the front desk, her movements distracted and overly precise, like she needed the task to keep her mind from unraveling. Her usual poise was replaced by a tightness in her jaw that betrayed how deeply she missed Lady Grey.

"We need to talk," Clara said. "Someone saw a man sneaking into the hedge maze the night Lady Grey disappeared."

"Vincent?"

Clara shrugged. "Fits the description."

Minutes later, they stood at the hedge maze entrance on the festival grounds. Lavender lined the walkways, filling the air with a calming fragrance. But Clara was focused on more than flowers. She crouched low, brushing her fingers over the trampled grass.

"Found something," she said.

She held up a black fiber. Wool. Possibly from a coat.

Inside the maze, they moved slowly, noting every bend and alcove. Near the center, an urn stood on a stone plinth. Clara peered inside and pulled out a note.

"Curiosity cuts deeper than silence. Stop digging."

Amelia paled. "The same font."

Clara folded the paper. "Someone's getting nervous."

Back at the inn, Clara spread out old maps of Tumblebrook from the shop's attic. One showed an underground springhouse beneath where the maze now stood. She underlined its entrance.

"If someone used the maze for a meeting spot, they'd need to know this."

That afternoon, Clara returned to the maze in disguise—a floppy hat, a clipboard, and an air of practiced nonchalance that masked the storm beneath her calm expression. Her stomach twisted with a mixture of dread and adrenaline, the same gnawing urgency that had haunted her since Lady Grey vanished. As she stepped into the maze's shaded entrance, the lavender scent was almost too sweet, cloying in a way that made her skin prickle.

Every sound—the crunch of her shoes on gravel, the rustle of hedges, the distant laughter from the festival—seemed amplified. Clara scanned the paths not just with her eyes but with a sixth sense born of desperation. She paused often, trailing fingers along leaves, crouching to examine subtle disturbances in the soil. A distant violin began to play, casting a strange elegance over the maze. The shadows stretched longer with the angle of the sun, turning familiar corners into ominous turns.

She caught a glint of something metallic near a hedge base. A bootprint. Large, fresh, and unmistakably adult. Her pulse quickened.

Nearby, a scrap of newspaper fluttered from a branch. She plucked it free and unfolded it. An obituary. E. Greaves—an old name connected to the Monarch Society.

Clara stood still, the paper trembling in her hand. The past wasn't just whispering through the maze. It was pressing in.

Later that evening, she and Amelia pieced it all together. When Clara showed the clipping, Amelia turned pale.

"He owned the land next to the maze."

Clara nodded. "Someone's stirring up buried business."

The mystery deepened, and Clara felt the chill of old secrets brushing against her spine. But she also felt something else: resolve. Whoever had taken Lady Grey had tangled with the wrong pair of women. And Clara was just getting started.

Chapter 7

The Gardener's Whispers

The early morning air in Tumblebrook was laced with the scent of fresh soil and marigolds, the dew still clinging to flower petals like tiny glass beads. Amelia Farnsworth stood on the back porch of the inn, sipping a cup of tea she had reheated twice but never quite finished. Her eyes swept the festival grounds, lingering on the vibrant chaos of the garden displays. Volunteers bustled about with watering cans and rakes, laughter floating through the air like pollen. But none of it felt right—not without Lady Grey.

The hollow absence of her feline companion pressed against her chest like a heavy vase with no flowers in it. Mornings had lost their rhythm. The inn had lost its soul. Lady Grey had been her shadow, her anchor—and without her, Amelia felt adrift.

She took another sip, grimaced at the lukewarm taste, and set the mug down on the railing. Today marked the third day since Lady Grey had vanished from the floral showcase. Though Amelia had put on a pleasant face for guests, her insides twisted tighter with each passing hour. Sleep had eluded her, replaced by mental loops of what-if scenarios, half-formed theories, and the echo of Lady Grey's meow.

She turned as someone approached. Melvin Grubb, the festival's eccentric gardener, ambled up the stone path with a watering pail in one hand and a sunflower-printed bandana knotted around his head like a pirate. His boots squelched in the damp grass, and he hummed an off-key tune that sounded suspiciously like a sea shanty.

"Morning, Miss Farnsworth," he said with a tip of his faded straw hat. "You look like you've seen a ghost."

"More like I haven't seen one," she replied, trying to summon a smile. "Any luck finding new leads?"

Melvin leaned in conspiratorially. "Depends what you're lookin' for. But I did see something odd yesterday."

Amelia perked up. "Odd? Do tell."

Melvin wiped his hands on his overalls and glanced around theatrically. "It's about them pawprints."

"Pawprints?" she repeated, her pulse ticking up.

"Yes ma'am. Cat-sized. Not dog. Out by my toolshed. They went right up to the back wall—then poof. Gone." He paused for effect. "But here's the kicker: when I went to show the prints to my assistant, the dirt'd been swept clean. Not a single print left."

Amelia's mouth went dry. "When was this?"

"Late afternoon, just after the brass band finished their rehearsal. Thought it was strange, but I've seen stranger things in this town. Still, figured I ought to mention it."

She nodded. "You did the right thing, Melvin."

They walked together toward the toolshed, a squat structure painted a cheerful mint green with creeping vines curling along the trim. It was wedged between the compost bins and a tall stand of sunflowers—nearly hidden unless you knew to look. As they walked, Melvin chatted about soil acidity, tulip pests, and the mystery of disappearing garden gloves.

Amelia crouched by the shed's rear corner. The soil looked

freshly disturbed. She ran her fingers gently over it, hoping to feel something—a residual warmth, an impression. Anything.

"You sure no one else was back here?"

Melvin shook his head. "Only person with a key's me, and I've been keepin' it in my sock since the festival started. Don't trust lockers."

She almost laughed but focused instead on the ground. The dirt was a darker shade, as though someone had hastily poured water over it. No visible prints remained, but something about the scene itched at her instincts.

Melvin stepped inside and emerged a moment later holding a muddy trowel. "Here—found this inside with fresh dirt still clingin' to it. Someone used it, but I swear I haven't touched it since Tuesday."

Amelia accepted it with a cloth and held it up. The trowel smelled faintly of lavender. "Clara said something about the eastern maze path being lined with lavender."

"Ah, those bushes were bloomin' crazy this year," Melvin said. "Could hide a rabbit in 'em. Or a cat, come to think of it."

A chill crept up Amelia's spine.

Back at the inn, she met Clara in the parlor and relayed everything. Clara opened her notebook, flipping to the page where she had documented the maze.

"Look at this path here—see how it circles near the shed? If Lady Grey was hiding or running, that's a natural direction. But why would someone wipe away the prints afterward?"

"Because they didn't want anyone knowing she'd been there," Amelia said. "Or worse—someone planted them."

The idea settled between them, heavy and unwelcome.

Amelia walked to the window, arms crossed. Beyond the glass, the town bustled with color and motion. Children ran with butterfly nets. A vendor shouted about lemonade. Somewhere, a violin began to play. It was all so normal—except it wasn't.

She turned back. "I want to talk to Vincent Pike. He's been too helpful. Too... precise."

Clara nodded. "He could've known the shed was close to the maze. Knew you'd be distracted running the inn. It's convenient."

But before they could act, a knock came at the door.

Melvin again—this time with something clutched in his hand.

"I nearly forgot," he said, breathless. "Found this wedged under a loose board in the shed wall. Looked like trash, but it's got writin'."

He handed over a torn piece of parchment—decorative, water-damaged, and smeared with soil. But the writing was clear:

Second bloom hides the gate. Do not trust the roots that grow beneath the gardener's name.

Clara read it twice, brow furrowed. "What does that even mean?"

"Sounds like a riddle," Amelia murmured. "But meant for who?"

Melvin shifted on his feet. "Could be it's part of that old garden society nonsense. You know, the Monarch types. They loved riddles, secret codes, blooming schedules. Too secretive, if you ask me."

Amelia blinked. "Wait—second bloom. Could that be a metaphor? Or maybe a literal planting cycle?"

Clara's eyes widened. "Or an actual second planting. What's in bloom now, Melvin?"

Melvin scratched his chin. "Well, tulips finished last week. But the double hollyhocks are starting their second bloom. Right over near the statue garden."

That was something. They thanked Melvin and headed toward the statue garden. The walk was a blur—Amelia's thoughts racing, hands fidgeting with her sweater sleeves.

The statue garden was tucked behind the conservatory, a winding trail flanked by wild roses and iron gates. Here, the hollyhocks indeed bloomed again—deep magentas and pale pinks rising like spires beside stone effigies.

It didn't take long. Clara pointed. "There—see the soil disturbance near the bench?"

Beneath the petals, a small stone slab had been shifted. Amelia knelt and tugged it aside, uncovering a hollow pocket filled with mulch and—something wrapped in waxed cloth.

She unwrapped it carefully. Inside: a tiny bell collar, unmistakably Lady Grey's.

Amelia gasped, breath catching in her throat. "She was here. She must've escaped—or someone planted this."

The moment felt heavy, hopeful, terrifying.

But they weren't alone. A twig snapped behind them. Both women whirled.

No one there. Just a shimmer of movement at the edge of the path.

Amelia clutched the collar, voice low. "We're close, Clara. I can feel it."

And behind them, a pair of golden eyes blinked once from the thicket—gone before they could turn.

Chapter 8

A Shadowy Holding

The world smelled wrong.

Lady Grey crouched low in the corner of a dim, shed-like structure, her sleek body tense and ears twitching with every creak of timber and rustle of wind through the warped boards. Dampness clung to the air, tinged with mold, rust, and the sharp scent of something chemical—fertilizer, perhaps. But beneath all that was the unmistakable aroma of lilies, crushed underfoot and fading fast. The same scent had lingered on the hands of the person who had taken her.

Her amber eyes flared in the half-light, tracking the faint movement of shadows beyond the slatted wall. The space was small—claustrophobically so—with only one grimy window set high in the wall and a rusted latch sealing the crooked door. Dust coated the floorboards, and boxes stacked haphazardly around her bore faded labels: SEEDLINGS. TWINE. LIME. Old garden posters clung to the walls like curled autumn leaves, their once-vibrant colors now dulled to sepia tones.

She had tested the perimeter twice. No gaps wide enough to squeeze through. The door was locked from the outside. She'd spent the first hour pacing the edges, brushing her cheek against each surface, pressing her paws into corners, and—when frustration reached its peak—letting out a mournful yowl that echoed pitifully in the stillness.

No one had answered.

But Lady Grey was not a creature easily defeated.

With slow, deliberate steps, she padded to the far corner where a floorboard seemed looser than the rest. Earlier, she'd noticed how her weight shifted oddly there—how the board gave slightly beneath her paws. She crouched and began working at it again, claws slipping into the grain, tugging and prying.

A sliver lifted.

She paused and sniffed. Air. Faint and cool. Something from outside. Encouraged, she returned to scratching, methodically peeling back the board just enough to slide something through.

Lady Grey paused, then twisted her body to groom a paw, dislodging a small tuft of fur that had clung stubbornly to her leg since the abduction. She gently batted it toward the gap and watched as the grey tuft drifted through the narrow space, vanishing into the sliver of light.

But she wasn't done.

She padded back to a crate marked ROSE FERTILIZER and nudged aside a shallow pile of dusty burlap. There, half-buried in the corner, was a small brass garden medallion—one she had managed to snag from her captor's coat in the initial scuffle. She'd kept it hidden, instinct telling her it might matter.

The medallion was round, etched with an emblem: a butterfly over crossed garden tools—eerily similar to the Monarch Society sigil Clara had once described aloud.

Carefully gripping the medallion in her teeth, she brought it back to the loosened floorboard. She hesitated only a moment before letting it drop from her mouth. The medallion skidded forward and clinked once against the wood before disappearing through the gap.

Someone would find it.

She just had to wait—and stay hidden when needed. Because she wasn't entirely alone. No, there were footsteps. Muffled, infrequent, but real. And each time they came, she retreated to the shadows, tail low, breath silent. The scent of her captor was distinct—cologne-tinged soil and crushed lilies—and it always preceded the soft rattle of keys and the groan of the outer door.

But they hadn't come in. Not yet. They seemed to check, hesitate, then leave.

Lady Grey suspected they were waiting. For what, she couldn't be sure. But she'd noticed something else—something strange.

Each time after the footsteps faded, a low hum would begin. Not quite mechanical, but rhythmic. A vibration through the floorboards. Water? Machinery? Or worse—something meant to unsettle her?

But Lady Grey wasn't afraid. She was calculating.

She leapt gracefully onto a box stack, peering through the slats toward the narrow slice of sky beyond the window. Somewhere out there, Amelia was searching. Clara too, no doubt with that sharp little notebook of hers. They would come. She only needed to leave enough crumbs.

To pass the time, she listened. Lady Grey had always been a keen observer. The birds outside chirped in odd rhythms—one that repeated every fifteen minutes or so. A robin? No. Too tinny. Too regular. Was it a recording? A distraction to mask other noises?

She lowered her head against the crate and concentrated.

Then it came again: a faint clang, metal against metal. A chain? A gate? A latch being tested, perhaps. Somewhere, someone was securing something. The rhythmic chirping resumed shortly after.

She climbed down and resumed pacing, not from anxiety, but from calculation. She'd begun memorizing the layout: the stack of broken pots near the door, the tarp-draped wheelbarrow along the east wall, the pile of gardening magazines yellowed with age. She knew every creaky plank now.

She had even discovered a line of ants trailing from a crack beneath the wall to the underside of a compost bin—proof she wasn't buried entirely underground. A comfort.

Near the tarp, she found something new: an old seed satchel tucked into a drawer. It smelled of chamomile and damp paper, but more importantly, it had a tear. With careful paws, she pulled it open and found—dried marigold seeds. The same flowers from the festival. The symbolism wasn't lost on her.

Lady Grey batted the packet to the floorboard, nudging a few seeds into the opening. It wasn't much, but if Amelia found it, she'd understand. Marigolds had always lined the inn's entrance.

Twilight fell.

Through the narrow window, light shifted—amber to rose, rose to lavender. And with cooling air came the footsteps again. Softer now. Measured. The sound of someone used to sneaking.

Lady Grey slipped behind the wheelbarrow and stilled. The door latch jiggled. Not opened—just tested. A pause. Then footsteps retreating.

But this time, they left something.

A low scrape against the boards. A whisper of movement near the threshold. She crept forward when silence returned and sniffed.

A folded piece of cloth, shoved through the door gap.

She sniffed again—ginger, rosemary... lemon balm? A handkerchief from the inn's kitchen? Had Clara sent it? Or was it a trick?

Carefully, she pawed it closer. Embroidered in the corner were initials—A.F.

Amelia.

Lady Grey sat down and blinked slowly. They were close.

But something had changed.

That night, as wind hissed through the walls, Lady Grey awoke to voices. Muffled and urgent. Not her captor's voice—this was a woman's, clipped and familiar. Then another—lower, uncertain.

She pressed her ear to the wall, straining.

"...tonight. We move her tonight. Before anyone else finds her."

Her fur bristled.

She wasn't being kept here for long. This shed was just a stop.

Lady Grey crept back to her floorboard. The tuft of fur was gone. The medallion too. Hopefully someone had seen them. Hopefully someone was following the trail.

She looked toward the cloth scrap again. Ginger, rosemary, lemon balm.

Hope.

Chapter 9

Into the Greenhouse

Clara Henderson pressed herself against the cool brick wall outside Melvin Grubb's greenhouse, her breath catching in her throat. The air carried the sharp scent of crushed thyme and freshly watered soil, mingled with the more unsettling whiff of mildew and metal. The greenhouse sat at the back of Melvin's property, shadowed by overgrown lilac bushes and an ancient maple tree whose twisting branches creaked with secrets. Clara's chest tightened. She wasn't just here as an investigator tonight —she was here as a friend, desperate to bring Lady Grey home.

Amelia Farnsworth crouched nearby, one hand braced against a weathered potting bench, the other gripping a slim flashlight with white-knuckled determination. Even in the partial moonlight, Clara could see the tightness around her friend's eyes—the steely mask of composure stretched thin over a core of worry.

"Ready?" Amelia whispered, her voice barely rising above the chirring of late-night crickets.

Clara gave a small nod, her mouth twitching with dry humor. "If we get caught, you're explaining this to the town council."

Amelia flashed a smirk, though her grip didn't ease. "If we get caught, we'll say it's an herb emergency. Emergency basil. You know how it is."

The tension broke just enough for a shared glance of mischief—familiar and grounding. Then, business resumed.

The greenhouse door wasn't locked. That alone sent a shiver through Clara. Melvin, despite his eccentricities, was notorious for padlocking everything from toolboxes to seed bins. For this place to be left unsecured after he'd claimed to see something suspicious? Too convenient.

Clara slowly pushed the door open. It creaked, the hinges wailing like a warning. Inside, the atmosphere changed. Humidity wrapped around them like a damp wool blanket. The air was thick with the fragrances of basil, rosemary, and dill—but beneath that was a metallic edge. And underneath it, the musty rot of something long wet and forgotten.

Melvin's greenhouse was a blend of whimsy and disorder. Ferns drooped from overhead baskets, their fronds brushing shoulders. Tomato seedlings stretched beneath flickering grow lights. Ceramic gnomes leaned at drunken angles beside cracked watering cans. But tonight, it felt staged. Carefully chaotic. As if someone had restored the mess to its familiar disarray after disturbing it.

Clara stepped inside first. Her boots sank slightly into the loose soil coating the tile floor. Amelia followed, sweeping the flashlight's beam across rows of hanging baskets and climbing vines.

Clara made her way to the back of the greenhouse, toward the area Melvin had indicated in his earlier ramblings. According to him, he'd seen pawprints—small, feline prints—leading toward the tool shed. But now? Nothing.

"It's been scrubbed," Clara muttered, kneeling to run a finger along the floorboard. The wood was damp, and the faint tang of bleach clung to it. "Scrubbed hard. Someone didn't just clean this area—they sterilized it."

Amelia joined her, eyes wide. "But he said they were right here."

"Then someone didn't want them seen again," Clara said, rising.

Her tone was steady, but her stomach twisted. The image of Lady Grey, locked in some hidden room, filled her with pressure that tightened her throat.

She turned to the potting bench. Its surface was meticulously neat—odd for Melvin, who usually organized by chaos theory. A small collection of garden tools lay to one side: pruning shears, a trowel, an unlabeled spray bottle. Next to them sat a spool of twine and—a scrap of fabric.

Clara picked it up carefully, heart thudding. The frayed edges and familiar gray hue confirmed it.

"Lady Grey," she whispered.

Amelia leaned in, her breath hitching. "She was here. Recently."

Clara's mind raced. "Why bring her here at all? Why not keep her in the woods or a basement?"

"Unless," Amelia said, brow furrowing, "this wasn't a hiding place. It was a transfer point."

A pass-off. The thought chilled Clara.

She straightened and scanned the room. Her eyes landed on a tall, slightly crooked cabinet wedged between two rain barrels.

She moved to it and opened the door.

Inside was the usual mess—bottles of fertilizer, old gloves, half-used plant tags. But nestled in the corner was a wooden box, etched with the butterfly sigil of the Monarch Society.

Clara lifted it out and brushed away a fine layer of dust. The box creaked slightly as she opened it.

Inside lay two items: a packet of marigold seeds and a folded piece of parchment.

She opened the paper slowly. A watercolor sketch of a garden medallion filled one side. On the other, in looping script:

Where the lilies weep, the path begins.

Amelia read over her shoulder. "That's not just a clue. It's a message."

Clara nodded, mind rifling through places in Tumblebrook with lilies—real and symbolic. "They're daring us to follow."

She closed the box and tucked it under her arm. Amelia gently pocketed the scrap of fur.

"She's still alive," Amelia said softly. "She has to be."

The unmistakable crunch of gravel outside sent both women into motion.

"Back entrance," Clara hissed.

They darted through the narrow walkway to a rear door hidden behind a curtain of ivy. Just as Amelia pulled it closed, a flashlight beam swept across the greenhouse entrance.

Melvin's silhouette filled the doorway, humming a folksy tune. He lingered, peered in, then wandered off.

Amelia pressed a hand to her chest. "Do you think he's involved?"

Clara shook her head. "No. But someone's using him. Just like they're using the garden festival. And us."

They crouched behind a hedge, watching as Melvin vanished into the dark, whistling.

The walk back to the inn was slow, careful. Every snapped branch made Clara tense, every wind gust sounded like footsteps. But her mind was sharper now. The game had changed.

As they approached the rear veranda, Clara looked again at the box. Marigold seeds. A medallion sketch. A cryptic clue. Everything pointed to planning—not desperation.

Back in the inn's warm kitchen, they set the box on the table between them.

Clara leaned over it, tapping the parchment. "'Where the lilies weep.' That's not just poetic. There's a place on the old town maps."

Amelia blinked. "The old chapel garden? The one that floods every spring?"

Clara's eyes lit up. "Exactly. Locals call it the Lily Bowl."

Amelia leaned forward, her voice tinged with wonder. "That has to be the next spot."

Clara nodded. "Tomorrow, we search the Lily Bowl. Tonight, we document everything."

She flipped open her notebook to a fresh page, her mind already sorting the puzzle into columns. But beneath her logic, a knot of dread sat heavy in her stomach.

This wasn't just a garden prank or petty ransom.

It was a message.

And someone in Tumblebrook was waiting for them to find it.

Chapter 10

A Note in the Night

Amelia Farnsworth had always found something soothing about the evening quiet of the Tumblebrook Inn. The clink of teacups in the drying rack, the muted rustle of curtains drawn against the chill, and the soft hum of Clara humming absentmindedly from the parlor—it was a comforting orchestration of calm. But tonight, every creak in the floorboards felt amplified. Every gust of wind against the windows carried with it a low, haunting note of unease.

She stood at the front desk, absently flipping through the guest registry, though her mind was far from the names and room numbers inked on the page. The box from Melvin's greenhouse sat beside her, its butterfly sigil half-covered by a doily, as if modesty could erase its significance. On the table lay the scrap of fur and the watercolor clue —both too damning to ignore and too fragile to display.

Lady Grey had been there. Had been moved. And someone wanted them to know.

Clara had gone upstairs to check the attic for any matching medallions to the one sketched in the note. Amelia, meanwhile, tried to appear busy in case anyone from town happened to walk in.

Festival guests had mostly gone to bed, their laughter replaced by a humming silence as the clock neared midnight. The Tumblebrook Garden Festival had always brought a cozy magic to spring, but this year's atmosphere had shifted—quietly but unmistakably.

The inn's front door rattled gently, a breeze catching the handle. But Amelia had locked it hours ago. She set the registry down and stepped over, her slippers quiet against the rug.

Something white caught her eye. Just inside the door, curled against the wood like a dropped napkin.

She crouched and picked it up—a slip of heavy paper, thick as cardstock.

There were no markings on the outside, no address or name.

She unfolded it slowly, her heart beginning to thud.

Block letters, typed—not handwritten:

This isn't about the cat. It's about the land beneath her paws.

Amelia read it three times. Then a fourth.

A cold thread of confusion slid down her spine. She turned toward the hallway, half-expecting Clara to be standing there with a sly grin, as if this were some twisted joke.

But no one was there.

She glanced at the lock on the door. Still engaged. The windows hadn't been opened. Whoever left the note had done it silently, quickly, and with purpose.

She hurried to the kitchen and placed the note beside the box, drawing in a sharp breath.

Clara returned a minute later, dust streaking one cheek, a rolled blueprint tube in her hand. "I think I found the original map—"

"Clara," Amelia interrupted, her voice tight. "Look."

Clara leaned over the table, reading the note.

A long silence followed.

Then Clara asked, "Land? What land?"

Amelia shook her head. "All I know is this isn't just a ransom. It never was."

They stared at the objects on the table: the Monarch Society box, the fur scrap, the cryptic watercolor clue—and now, the anonymous message.

Amelia murmured, "What did Lady Grey walk across that someone wants to keep hidden?"

Clara unrolled the blueprint tube and spread a worn, faded survey map across the kitchen table. "Let's find out."

The map, once pristine and prized, was now yellowed and curling. Fine inked lines detailed the property boundaries of old Tumblebrook: plots labeled with family names long faded from memory; waterways that had shifted; and roads now paved over with time. But one section—just behind the Tumblebrook Inn—was circled faintly in pencil.

"Look here," Clara said, pointing near the map's edge. "This ridge runs behind the inn and curves toward what used to be the orchard."

Amelia leaned in. "Lady Grey always stops there. She's always drawn to that spot."

Clara narrowed her eyes. "It was once part of the Farnsworth property, but... see this? A marginal note: 'Survey discrepancy – boundary undefined.'"

Amelia sat back, folding her hands tightly. "Could someone be trying to claim it? Is that why they took her—to distract us while something else is happening?"

Clara traced the pencil line. "This irregular boundary—if someone wanted to develop or claim ownership, this old survey might be the only proof of your rights."

Amelia shook her head. "But who would go through all this trouble... over a patch of hillside?"

"Someone who knows what's underneath it," Clara said.

The clock chimed once, startling them both.

They turned to the window. Outside, the town slept—porch lights flickered like fireflies, and the festival booths sat empty, canvas flaps rustling in the breeze.

Amelia reached for the note again. "This isn't about the cat. It's about the land beneath her paws."

The phrasing unsettled her. Not just the message itself, but the language. It didn't feel like a threat—it sounded almost... ritualistic.

"What if it's not just about ownership?" she said. "What if it's about history—something someone wants to rewrite or erase?"

Clara tapped the Monarch Society box. "Then we need to learn what they're hiding. And fast."

They stayed at the kitchen table past midnight, making notes, comparing maps, building a timeline. They pored over guest logs, old newspaper clippings, and even one of the Farnsworth family journals, hunting for clues to secrets buried beneath the inn.

Through it all, Amelia struggled to stay composed. But her thoughts looped endlessly: Lady Grey, missing. The note's clipped warning. Her own trembling hands.

By the time they turned in, exhaustion dulled Amelia's thoughts. But sleep wouldn't come easily.

Her dreams were strange and fragmented. Lady Grey, pacing behind invisible fences. Flowers blooming over stone. The whisper of wind murmuring: "Beneath her paws. Beneath her paws."

At dawn, Amelia awoke with a start. One thought burned in her mind: she had to speak with Doris Finch. If anyone knew about old land claims—or buried town gossip—it was Doris. The café owner had been around long enough to know which whispers held weight.

As Amelia padded across the inn's quiet floor to make tea, she glanced again at the mysterious note on the counter.

It was still there. Heavy in its simplicity.

Somewhere out there, Lady Grey was still missing.

And now Amelia knew—they weren't just searching for a cat.

They were uncovering a secret buried beneath their very feet.

Chapter 11

Check the Boundaries

Clara Henderson prided herself on being grounded. She wasn't prone to romanticizing the past or entertaining conspiracies. Her mind worked in logic—in lines and margins, in neatly annotated notebooks and thoughtfully constructed timelines. But as she stared down at the antique maps spread across the Tumblebrook Inn's kitchen table, even she had to admit—something strange was unraveling. Not just curious-strange, but town-defining strange. The kind that didn't whisper mystery but shouted it with a bullhorn and left cat fur and cryptic notes in its wake.

The typed message from the night before still lay beside her elbow:

This isn't about the cat. It's about the land beneath her paws.

Clara reread it for the fifth time as Amelia stirred honey into her tea. Each clink of the spoon echoed in the silence. The kettle hissed in the background. Curtains swayed gently in the breeze. Outside, the Tumblebrook Garden Festival was beginning to stir—early risers bustling between booths, vendors hammering down signs, music warming up in broken chords. But inside the inn's kitchen, tension hung thick.

Clara pushed her glasses up the bridge of her nose and turned back to the attic map she'd retrieved the night before. Its survey lines wavered—especially around the ridge behind the inn, one of Lady Grey's favorite haunts. Faint pencil notes hinted at inconsistencies: a boundary shifted by inches, a vague remark—survey incomplete.

"It's not just the land," Clara murmured. "It's what's under it."

Amelia leaned closer, her expression tight. "That ridge has always been ours. Great-Aunt Annie had a garden path there. We used to bury time capsules as kids."

Clara tapped the map. "But look at this—the boundary line shifts from this 1918 plat to the 1954 survey. Only by a few feet, but enough. If someone wanted to exploit a gray area in land ownership, that shift might be just enough to give them legal leverage."

"And if they knew we wouldn't be paying attention," Amelia said, voice hardening, "they could move in without anyone noticing."

Clara nodded. "And if they needed a distraction—"

Amelia finished, "—they'd take Lady Grey."

Silence fell.

For a long moment, they both stared at the map. The paper was brittle, the ink faded, but the implications were sharp. Clara slowly traced a route along the ridge line with the eraser end of a pencil. "If someone's using the catnapping to keep us busy, they're working fast. I need to know who's been watching this land."

She stood, rolling several maps and tucking them into her satchel. "I'm going to the bookshop. Mr. Lark keeps property records in the back. If there's any paperwork—sales, disputes, old plans—I'll find it."

"Let me come with—" Amelia began.

"You stay here," Clara said gently. "In case Lady Grey returns. Or in case someone tries something else. If they're this bold, they might come back."

Clara stepped into the vibrant chaos of the festival. Flower crowns bobbed atop visitors' heads. Children darted between stalls. The air was thick with roasted lavender almonds and damp earth.

But to Clara, it all felt too bright, too busy, too loud—like the town was performing distraction.

She paused at the hedge maze near the inn. Something about it looked... altered. One pathway had been trimmed hastily, unevenly. She snapped a photo and moved on.

Gossamer Fables was blissfully quiet. Mr. Lark stood at a display table, arranging a tower of seed catalogues.

"Clara! Here for your usual mystery fix?"

"Only if it includes historic zoning regulations," she replied.

His eyes twinkled. "Back office. Bottom drawer. The one labeled 'Eminent Domain Drama.'"

Clara dove in.

An hour later, she'd found a 1926 deed transfer with a red X over the ridge and a cryptic note: Future Excavation Site – Pending Approval. Her pulse quickened. Another file from the 1950s documented a halted project after community objections—and a familiar phrase: Monarch Society petition successfully blocked development.

A final folder revealed a heated exchange between two town council members, including Horace Pike. Clara circled the name and photographed every relevant document.

She texted Amelia: Found evidence. Meet me at the café. Bring gloves. And coffee.

At the café, they huddled in the corner booth, backs to the wall.

"Doris," Clara said, "did you ever hear stories about digging or construction behind the inn?"

Doris leaned in. "My father said there were tunnels. Old bootlegger routes from the river to the orchards. When the Monarchs got wind of it, they sealed it all up. Called it preservation."

Amelia went pale. "Could there still be something down there?"

"Wouldn't be the first time secrets were buried beneath roses," Doris said.

That afternoon, Clara and Amelia hiked past the garden and up the ridge. The path was mostly overgrown. At the ridge's base, Clara spotted a depression in the brush. She pushed aside vines—and gasped.

A narrow wooden hatch lay flush with the earth.

Amelia knelt beside her. "I thought it was just a cellar door."

Clara lifted the hatch. Ancient-smelling air wafted out—moss, damp stone, and something older. Brick-framed stairs led downward, tangled with roots. Above the passage, a metal butterfly was etched in the arch.

Clara stepped back, breath shallow. "This is what they wanted. This passage. This space."

Amelia nodded. "This is what Lady Grey found."

They stared into the darkness. A whisper of cold air rose from below.

"Tomorrow," Clara said. "We come back. Prepared."

For the first time, Clara felt the lines on the map beginning to connect—not just ink and paper, but a trail. One someone had tried very hard to erase.

Chapter 12

The Chamber Beneath

The wind rustled low through the pines as Amelia and Clara stood once again at the ridge's edge, the earth still damp from spring rains. The narrow wooden hatch lay nestled among moss and stone, exactly as they'd left it days ago—unassuming, unmarked, and hiding something far older than either of them had anticipated.

"No sign of anyone since?" Clara asked, scanning the treeline.

"None," Amelia replied. "I've been checking it every morning. It's like the whole town forgot this place existed."

Clara brushed away pine needles and knelt beside the hatch. "Which probably means it's exactly where we need to be."

Amelia steadied her breath as the hinges creaked and the hatch lifted. The cool scent of soil and cedar drifted up from the opening, laced with something subtler—old paper, maybe, or ink that had been waiting decades to be read.

The flashlight beam cut into the darkness below, revealing a narrow spiral staircase carved into stone.

They descended slowly, each footstep echoing off the damp

walls. The air thickened with every turn, the silence pressing close as they reached the bottom.

At the base was a small antechamber—no wider than the inn's sitting room—its walls lined with wooden shelves stacked with wax-sealed documents, leather-bound ledgers, and metal canisters etched with the faint, familiar butterfly crest of the Monarch Society.

A single table sat in the center, heavy with the weight of secrets. Papers fanned out across it—maps, typewritten memos, hand-inked annotations.

Clara moved first, brushing dust from the surface. "They were planning something big down here. Look—land surveys. Development grids. This one's dated two months ago."

Amelia lifted a ledger, its spine brittle, its contents organized by surname and symbol. Her eyes drifted to a name near the top of the list—**Annabelle Farnsworth**.

Her throat tightened. "She was down here."

Clara leaned over. "What does it say?"

Amelia opened the ledger to the marked page. It wasn't just a name. It was a title.

Initiates of Concord: Annabelle Farnsworth — Inner Circle, Ritual Overseer (1958–1974).

"That's not just membership," Clara murmured. "That's leadership."

"No," Amelia said quietly. "That's infiltration. Aunt Annie wasn't *with* them. She was *watching* them. Maybe trying to stop them."

Beneath Annie's title was a list of coded dates and phrases—some crossed out, others underlined. One in particular had been written several times in ink and pencil:

The tea ritual must be maintained.

Only through the tea is the memory retained.

Do not stop the tea.

Clara stared at it, eyebrows drawn. "Tea?"

Amelia nodded slowly. "Annie made a special blend. Said it

helped with clarity and sleep. I still brew it every week for guests. It's become... a tradition."

"But what if it's more than that?" Clara said. "If this 'ritual' is tied to memory, to truth—what if that tea was part of a... process?"

"A delivery method," Amelia said, voice barely above a whisper. "Or protection. Or... a trigger."

They exchanged a glance. Everything they knew—everything they'd assumed—had just shifted.

Clara reached for another folder but froze. A muffled thud echoed from above.

They both turned toward the stairwell. Heavy, deliberate footsteps.

The hatch groaned shut.

And the light from above disappeared.

* * *

Darkness engulfed the chamber. Their flashlights flickered, shadows dancing on the stone walls.

"Someone's up there," Clara whispered. "They closed us in."

"Which means they know we're here," Amelia said, pulse quickening.

Clara darted to the staircase and tried the hatch. "Locked. From the outside."

They stood in tense silence, the weight of the sealed chamber pressing in around them.

"We need another way out," Amelia said.

Clara scanned the chamber with renewed urgency. Her light passed over the far wall—stone etched with faint markings. She stepped closer.

"There's a seam here. Looks like another door."

Amelia joined her. The stone was set into a frame slightly recessed from the rest of the wall.

Clara felt along the grooves, then reached into a niche. Her fingers found a metal lever.

"Ready?" she asked.

Amelia nodded.

Clara pulled.

The stone door groaned open an inch. They pushed together, revealing a narrow passage just wide enough for one person at a time.

A gust of fresher air drifted through.

"It leads out," Amelia said. "It must."

They moved quickly, ducking into the hidden corridor. The walls were tighter here, the stone damp and slick. Their flashlights glinted off rusted sconces and broken tiles. Occasionally, faded Monarch symbols peeked through grime, reminders that this path had once been used often—and in secret.

"Whoever sealed us in didn't know about this exit," Clara murmured.

Or they hoped we wouldn't find it, Amelia thought.

The tunnel twisted downward, then began to climb. At last, they reached a wooden door bolted with a rusted latch. Clara shoved it open with her shoulder, grunting with the effort.

They spilled out into a grove behind the ridge, overgrown with bramble and vines. Amelia gulped fresh air as the sky—now awash in the amber of late afternoon—came into view.

"We need to move fast," Clara said. "If someone tried to trap us, they might still be nearby."

They scrambled down the slope toward Amelia's car, hidden off a service road. Her hands trembled as she turned the key in the ignition.

Only once they were back on the road did either of them speak.

"They knew we were close," Amelia said. "That we were onto Annie's part in all of this."

"And if the tea was part of it—if it really held some key to preserving memory..." Clara trailed off.

Amelia stared ahead, her mind racing. The blend had always

been passed down, unchanged. She made it just as Annie had shown her.

"What if that's why I've remembered things others haven't?" Amelia murmured. "Why clues kept coming to me?"

Clara turned slowly to look at her. "You mean the tea didn't just calm you. It kept the truth alive."

Amelia didn't answer. Her hands tightened around the wheel.

Back at the inn, she would need to do one thing immediately.

Check the tea.

And make sure no one had tampered with it.

Chapter 13

Tea with Trouble

Amelia Farnsworth had always believed in the sanctity of teatime. There was a rhythm to it—a comforting pause in the middle of the day that restored order to the mind and palate. Her great-aunt Annie used to say that any trouble could be managed better with a warm cup and a level gaze. But today, even her beloved ritual couldn't shake the gnawing unease curling through her gut.

The silver tea service gleamed on the parlor table, the china cups delicately clinking against their saucers, but her thoughts were anything but composed. Sunlight filtered through the lace curtains, casting golden rays across the room, yet it did nothing to ease the tension in her chest. She adjusted a vase of early spring blooms for the third time before finally settling into the armchair across from her newest guest.

Vincent Pike, the supposed charmer of Juniper Lane, sat with effortless poise. He looked perfectly at home in the inn's antique setting, dressed in a crisp white shirt and gray tweed blazer—equal parts catalog model and retired politician. He held his teacup like an aristocrat, swirling the Earl Grey with theatrical care before taking a measured sip.

Amelia watched him closely, reading between the polished gestures and too-perfect compliments. Something about his presence unsettled her—like the creak of a loose floorboard in a quiet room. She reminded herself this wasn't a social visit. This was a test.

"You've made this place shine, Amelia," Vincent said, offering a warm smile. "It's a marvel of small-town resilience. Historic, charming—prime, really."

There it was again—that strange emphasis. Amelia tilted her head, pretending to be amused. "Well, the inn's been in my family for generations. I'd hardly call it prime real estate."

Vincent's smile tightened. "Oh, I think you'd be surprised. Value isn't always about what's above the ground. Sometimes, it's what's beneath it."

Amelia blinked. Her fingers froze around the sugar spoon. "That's an interesting observation."

"Just something I picked up in my years working with land development," he said smoothly. "Old plots like these hold secrets. Value. Sometimes... opportunities."

She stirred her tea slowly, each clink of the spoon a metronome to her rising suspicion. "I wasn't aware you worked in development. I thought you were retired."

Vincent laughed—a breathy sound too rehearsed. "One never really retires from understanding the lay of the land. Especially when the lay is so curious."

They sipped in silence, the air between them thick with something unspoken. Amelia's eyes drifted to Lady Grey's favorite window perch —still empty. Her absence lingered like a wound that hadn't scabbed.

Vincent followed her gaze. "Still no sign of the cat?"

"No," she said shortly. "But we haven't stopped looking."

"I hope you find her soon," he said, setting his cup down. "Though sometimes, pets go missing for reasons beyond our comprehension."

Amelia smiled politely, steel sharpening beneath it. "Sometimes they're taken."

His brow lifted. "Surely not."

"Vincent," she said, leaning forward, "what exactly brought you to Tumblebrook?"

He chuckled, settling back in the armchair. "A need for peace. For simplicity. Isn't that what brings most people here?"

She nodded slowly. "And yet you seem very interested in what's buried beneath my land."

He waved a hand. "Idle curiosity. Nothing more."

Amelia rose to refill the teapot—more to place space between them. She carried the pot to the tray, her fingers tightening on the handle. Idle curiosity. The phrase echoed in her aunt's journals—often describing Monarch Society visitors.

"Do you believe in local legends, Vincent? Secret tunnels? Societies buried in old brick?"

"Every town has its fairy tales," he said. "Doesn't mean they're not rooted in truth."

Amelia returned with the pot. "And would you say you've found truth here?"

Vincent's eyes sparkled. "Let's just say I've found potential."

He rose to inspect a framed map above the mantel, lingering on the lines marking the inn's boundary. "Did you know some of these plots haven't been surveyed in over a century? Fascinating what's left out of the records."

Amelia forced a light laugh. "Are you suggesting I've been squatting on hidden treasure, Mr. Pike?"

He turned with a grin. "Wouldn't that be something?"

* * *

That evening, the inn quieted to a hush, guests tucked into their rooms. In the small library, Amelia and Clara pored over survey maps, deeds, and weathered blueprints spread like a spider's web of secrets.

"He knows something," Amelia said flatly.

Clara flipped through zoning records. "He's dropping hints like breadcrumbs—but too polished, too deliberate. He's playing a game."

Amelia tapped a 1924 map. "He talked about what's under the land. That's not something tourists bring up."

Clara pointed to a faded ledger entry. "Here—'ridge shaft, abandoned, sealed by council order.' Matches the spot he kept eyeing during your tea."

"Lady Grey's disappearance, the note, now Vincent's insinuations —it all connects."

"The Monarch Society may not be as defunct as everyone thinks," Clara said. "What if they've been maneuvering to reclaim land lost nearly a century ago?"

Silence fell as the grandfather clock chimed ten. Candlelight flickered against the wood-paneled walls, making the quiet feel heavier.

Clara shifted a map and revealed an envelope. "Addressed to your great-aunt Annie. It's unopened."

Amelia opened it with shaking hands. Inside was a warning: "They want the ground. Not what grows on it. Not who lives on it. Protect the inn."

Her breath caught. "Clara..."

Clara reached for the document. "It's real. They've been circling back for decades."

A sharp knock at the door startled them. Amelia rushed down. A small, nondescript parcel lay on the step. No name. No note.

Inside, nestled in cotton, was a broken Monarch butterfly pin— and a tuft of gray fur.

Amelia's knees nearly buckled. "Lady Grey..."

Clara appeared, eyes narrowing. "They're taunting us. This is personal."

Amelia's voice hardened. "Then we stop being careful. We fight back. We protect this place—just like Aunt Annie did."

Upstairs, Amelia packed the documents into a canvas bag. She glanced at the broken pin—its cracked wings still intact, a fractured emblem of warning and truth.

She looked toward the darkened window. Somewhere out there, Lady Grey was still waiting. And so was the truth, buried beneath roots, stone, and silence.

The battle for the inn, for Lady Grey—and for Tumblebrook—had just begun.

Chapter 14

The Permit Problem

Morning sunlight spilled through the broad windows of Gossamer Fables, casting warm stripes across the polished oak floor. Clara Henderson adjusted her spectacles and carefully balanced a tray of blueberry scones beside the register. The clink of ceramic cups and the scent of baking should have created a tranquil morning—but Clara's thoughts were far from calm.

She hadn't slept. Not truly. The broken Monarch Society pin, the tuft of Lady Grey's fur left like a signature in the night—it all looped through her mind. Her dreams had been uneasy things: flickering shadows, vanishing cats, crumbling blueprints turning to ash in her hands. By sunrise, she'd given up on sleep, her nerves frayed as if from too much static.

Now, in the bookshop attic that doubled as an archive, she sought solace in logic. Dusty records, ledgers, and meticulously labeled boxes—this was her church. These were her hymns.

She was supposed to be inventorying rare gardening books for the Garden Festival, but her mind kept returning to Vincent Pike's visit. Specifically, what he'd said to Amelia about permits and land value.

Something didn't sit right. She hadn't voiced it at the time, but now it gnawed at her like an old splinter.

With a determined breath, she left the scone tray behind and climbed the narrow stairs to the attic. The slanted space smelled of cedar and aged paper, dust swirling in shafts of light that angled through dormer windows. The atmosphere wrapped around her like an old cardigan.

The green ledger labeled "Event Permits – Tumblebrook Annual Celebrations" was exactly where she remembered. She pulled it down gently and flipped to the latest entries.

Permit Issued: Town of Tumblebrook Festival Coordinator: Marion Brockwell Approval Stamp: TTB-1922-T

Clara frowned. "1922?"

That couldn't be right. She grabbed a more recent binder from 2022.

Permit Issued: Town of Tumblebrook Festival Coordinator: Marion Brockwell Approval Stamp: TTB-2022-G

Same coordinator. Same event. But this year's permit bore a stamp that hadn't been in use for over a century. Even the paper was subtly different—rougher, like something from an old municipal archive.

She dove deeper, pulling a dusty wooden box from a cabinet labeled "Misc. Zoning – Historic." Inside: brittle maps, faded memos, parchment envelopes sealed with yellowing wax.

One envelope, labeled MONARCH LAND USE – EASTERN PROPERTIES, bore the same 1922-T stamp.

Her heart stuttered. "It's not just an old stamp. It's theirs. The Monarch Society's."

She moved quickly now, clutching the suspicious documents and heading downstairs. Mr. Lark was arranging floral folklore books by region.

"Judging by your face," he said, "you've either solved a murder or found a stash of forbidden gardening catalogs."

"Worse." Clara laid the permits side by side on the counter. "This stamp—this one's forged. It's the same stamp used on Monarch Society land-use documents. The festival is technically unauthorized."

His jovial expression vanished. "Are you sure?"

"I double-checked. It's subtle but deliberate. If the event's being used to justify rezoning, it's built on forged approval."

He rubbed his beard. "And whoever did this had access to both municipal records and Monarch archives. That's a short list."

"Exactly. Vincent. Marion. Maybe a few others." Clara packed the evidence into her satchel. "I'm heading to town hall. I need to confirm whether this forgery made it into the official files."

Gossamer Fables faded behind her as she strode down Main Street. The morning sparkled with cheerful normalcy—shopfront windows gleaming, garden flags dancing in the breeze—but the color felt false now, too bright against the dark questions building in her mind.

Tumblebrook's town hall, a tidy brick building veiled in ivy, buzzed with low-level activity. Inside, Clara was greeted by the frustrated growl of a malfunctioning printer and the muttered curses of Miss Reenie Dalca.

"Paper jam number five," Reenie sighed. "If you're here about booth fees, give me a minute to battle the beast."

"I'm after festival permits," Clara said. "Last few years."

"Second office on the left," Reenie said. "Lower cabinet drawers. Watch out for dust dragons."

In the narrow office, Clara found the FESTIVALS drawer and pulled the folder for the current year. Her heart sank. The forged permit was there—same stamp, same formatting. No annotations. No corrections.

She let out a breath. Someone had replaced the official record.

As she closed the folder, a thin sheet slipped free. A graphite tracing. She unfolded it gently.

Property lines—faint but deliberate. The garden of the Tumblebrook Inn had been redrawn, extending into what was supposed to be public green space. Except here, it was labeled: Monarch Society Holdings.

Her pulse kicked. Someone was manipulating records—possibly to reclaim land under Amelia's feet.

She snapped photos, returned the files, and left town hall in a rush. The breeze had shifted cooler. At the garden festival, Vincent Pike laughed with Marion Brockwell near the coffee stand. He glanced her way, eyes flicking to her satchel.

Her pace quickened.

Back at the inn, Amelia was trimming tulips.

"We've got a problem," Clara said. "The festival permit is forged. The town's copy is fake. And someone redrew the land lines—your garden is marked as Monarch property."

Amelia froze, pruning shears suspended mid-air.

"They're using the festival as cover," Clara continued. "Lady Grey may have just been leverage to distract us."

Amelia stood slowly. "Then we look in the right direction."

Inside, the dining table had become their investigation headquarters. They spread out the permit copies, records, and graphite tracing. Clara pulled old town maps from her satchel.

The overlaps were undeniable.

"This proves it," Amelia whispered. "Someone is forging legal documents to reclaim Monarch land. And they're doing it under the guise of a garden festival."

They looked at each other. The catnapping wasn't a random act.

It was a diversion.

And beneath the cheerful banners and flowerbeds, someone was rewriting the boundaries of Tumblebrook.

Chapter 15

Woodland Escape

T he rusted hinges groaned open, their sound echoing into the night like the first note of a long-awaited symphony. Cold air rushed in, carrying with it the scent of freedom— and something older: damp stone and secrets.

Lady Grey darted from the shadowed corner of the toolshed, her sleek grey body slinking low to the ground. Each movement was deliberate, practiced, silent. For days, she had mapped every sound, every scent, every flicker of light that crept through the cracks in the old structure. The hooting owl in the rafters. The crunch of footsteps across gravel. The sharp tang of machine oil and the stale bitterness of tobacco that clung to the man who came and went, always muttering and pacing.

She had waited. Watched. Learned. Her patience had bloomed beyond instinct. It had become purpose. Each clawed tug at the slat beneath the workbench had been a protest, a promise. Tonight, it had finally given way.

Slipping through the narrow opening into the cool dark, her fur brushed against jagged wood. The air hit her like a wave: crisp, wild, alive. A thousand smells greeted her—pine, loam, wild onion, dew-wet grass, and woodsmoke from a distant chimney. She paused just long enough to confirm the tuft of fur and ribbon fragment remained —a breadcrumb of survival.

With a flick of her tail and the glint of resolve in her amber eyes, she vanished into the forest.

The Tumblebrook woods stretched vast and enigmatic—a shifting sea of silver and shadow under the moonlight. To most, they would be a maze of confusion. But to Lady Grey, they were memory. The scent of damp moss pulled at half-formed kittenhood recollections—the time Amelia carried her in a basket along the orchard path, the warmth of sun-warmed stone beneath her paws, the hush of trees breathing around her.

She moved with practiced grace, slipping through undergrowth and ducking beneath overhanging branches. The ground was cool and soft beneath her feet, the silence broken only by the sigh of wind and the rustle of unseen things. She followed a familiar sloping trail toward a hidden creek—a ribbon of silver whispering through the forest floor. She crouched to drink, her tongue lapping gently at the water, ears twitching with every rustle.

Then—a sound.

The softest crunch. A weight disturbing fallen leaves.

Lady Grey froze, muscles tensing. Her tail stiffened. She turned sharply and disappeared into a bramble, her movements soundless.

She ran until Widow's Rock loomed ahead—a pale boulder shrouded in moss and layered with memory. She paused, catching her breath. Then, rising on her hind legs, she scratched her mark into the mossy flank—four deliberate gashes.

A signal. Not just for Amelia or Clara, but for those who still remembered the old ways. The silent codes.

Leaping atop the stone, she scanned the woods. The inn lay beyond the treeline. Home. And danger.

The breeze shifted, and with it came that bitter metallic tang— motor oil, cologne, and something sharp. The man with the oil-soaked boots.

She hissed, low and quiet, before bounding down the opposite side of the rock.

Escape wasn't enough. She had to make it home. And she had to warn them.

She traveled deeper, weaving through deer paths and forgotten trails. The woods whispered as she passed—mouse scampers, moth wings, distant owl calls. Her world was painted in scent and sound. She passed the crooked sycamore where she once chased a squirrel to exhaustion. She scaled a tree, crouched tight against the limb. Below, a flashlight beam carved through the dark like a blade.

"She couldn't have gone far. Get the nets."

The voice rose from below. Lady Grey didn't move. Her breath stilled. Only when the man had passed did she descend, moving east toward the quarry trail.

There, past the moss-covered stone wall, lay the hidden entrance to Gossamer Fables' rear alley—a place of safety. Of allies.

But she wasn't safe yet.

Near the clearing by the glen, she caught a new scent. Fertilizer. She crouched beneath a hedge and peered into the greenhouse.

Inside, beneath flickering lanternlight, a figure paced. Another stood nearby, arms crossed. Broad-shouldered. Too polished for a gardener. Papers shifted. Voices murmured.

"I don't care about their stupid cat. The land's been rezoned. That's what matters."

Lady Grey crept backward, breath catching in her throat. She didn't need to know every word. The tone, the posture—it told her everything.

She turned and ran.

Past the mill ruins. Through mud and brambles. Her paws bled. Her legs trembled. But still she ran. At a blackberry thicket, her fur caught. She left another tuft behind.

A sign. A trail.

She climbed the cemetery wall. The moon hung high, illuminating the silhouette of the inn like a beacon.

Home.

She paused at the hydrangea along the back fence. Voices drifted from the patio, quiet and sharp.

"We have to move fast," one man whispered. "That cat's not just a pet. She knows the terrain. If she gets back—"

"Then we make sure she doesn't," another voice cut in. "The orchard's our best shot. That nosy girl's already digging into the deed boundaries."

Lady Grey's ears flattened.

"We've got the permits. Just need one more forged approval. Then the land's ours."

A cruel laugh. "And nobody's going to believe two nosy women and a cat."

A rustle. "Unless they find the original surveys. Or the tunnel."

Lady Grey's eyes narrowed.

Tunnel.

She bolted under the porch, slipping into the crawlspace she knew by heart. Her heart thundered, her chest rising and falling with exertion.

This was no longer about escape.

This was about returning.

She curled into a tight ball, body trembling with fatigue but eyes sharp. She would rest. And then she would act.

She wasn't just a missing cat anymore.

She was the key to everything buried beneath Tumblebrook.

And she had work to do.

Chapter 16

A Footprint Too Many

The air was thick with the scent of dew and pine when Amelia Farnsworth stepped off the back porch of the inn, a steaming thermos of hibiscus tea in one hand and Lady Grey's collar clutched in the other. She hadn't let go of it since finding it the night before, tangled in a patch of wild violet near the edge of town. The tiny bell was gone, the leather strap frayed. It felt like both a fragment of hope—and a warning.

"She's alive," Amelia whispered. "She has to be."

She crossed the herb garden and followed the winding path toward Widow's Rock. Clara had mentioned the mossy boulder—said she saw claw marks. At first it sounded far-fetched, but the idea that Lady Grey might have been clever enough to leave clues sparked something fragile but powerful inside Amelia: resolve.

Morning birdsong threaded through the trees, but even the gentle rhythms of the forest couldn't dispel the tension curling in Amelia's chest. Her boots crunched softly on the path. The forest, as always, breathed around her, serene and ancient.

Widow's Rock loomed ahead. She slowed her steps. Her gaze swept the area—and then paused.

A boot print.

Fresh. Deep. Not her own. The tread pattern was distinctive.

She knelt, studying it. Size eleven. Vibram sole. Clara had pointed out that same boot pattern in her notes just yesterday. And Vincent Pike had worn Vibram-soled hiking boots the day he brought that absurdly perfect basket of blueberries.

Amelia snapped a photo.

Then came the voice.

"Amelia?"

She stood abruptly, her heart leaping into her throat.

Vincent appeared at the edge of the clearing, hiking poles in hand, a satchel slung over his shoulder. His smile was immediate. Polished. Controlled.

"Didn't mean to startle you," he said. "Thought I'd catch the sunrise from the ridge."

She gestured to the print. "You already did."

He followed her gaze and chuckled. "Ah, yeah. Came through a couple days ago. Trail holds footprints longer this time of year."

Amelia raised a brow. "Convenient. Someone spotted movement near Melvin's greenhouse that same day. You wouldn't know anything about that, would you?"

Vincent's smile held, but his grip on the hiking poles tightened. "You're really committed to this cat search."

"She's not just a cat," Amelia replied. "She's family."

A flicker of something passed over his face—dismissiveness or irritation—but it vanished just as quickly. He tipped an invisible hat and turned toward the trail. "Well, best of luck."

Amelia watched until the trees swallowed him whole. Then she crouched again beside the print. Looking at the rock before her, she saw them.

Claw marks.

Her throat tightened. She took another photo and resumed circling the rock.

Near the western edge, half-hidden in damp fern, something caught the light.

A silver bell.

Amelia froze. The bell from Lady Grey's collar. She picked it up gently, her fingers trembling.

"You were here," she whispered. "You made it this far."

Back at the inn, she found Clara at the dining table, surrounded by maps, property records, and zoning documents. Amelia showed her the photos.

Clara leaned in. "That boot tread? New model. Less than a year old. Vincent was wearing those exact boots the day of the festival setup."

Amelia nodded. "He claims he was hiking."

"To Melvin's greenhouse? Funny, because the lock there's been tampered with."

They shared a look.

Amelia set down the bell. "She left us a trail."

Clara pulled out a land survey. "Remember that copy from the attic? The ridge near Widow's Rock? On current records it's listed as town-owned, but this version shows it under private ownership—a shell company."

"Vincent?"

Clara nodded. "Tied to him through a defunct real estate trust."

Amelia exhaled. "He's circling our land. And Lady Grey got too close."

They headed back to the trail that afternoon. The woods were quieter. As they reached the boulder again, Clara found fur snagged on a low-hanging bramble.

"Struggled," she murmured. "This wasn't a clean escape."

They followed more disturbed soil along a narrow footpath. Amelia stopped beside a birch. Something small caught her eye.

A button. Silver. Engraved.

Amelia picked it up, her breath shallow.

It matched the cufflinks on Vincent Pike's tailored coat.

Clara met her gaze. "We're closing in."

Amelia nodded, curling her fingers around the bell in her pocket. "So is she."

Chapter 17

Deeds and Doubts

The bell above the door of Gossamer Fables gave its usual cheerful chime as Clara stepped inside, brushing a light dusting of dried leaves from her shoulders. The air inside the bookshop offered a welcome contrast to the crisp breeze outside—warm, inviting, and steeped in the scent of paper, ink, and the ever-present pot of lavender tea that Mr. Lark insisted on simmering at the back counter.

Today, Clara didn't pause to exchange pleasantries. Her thoughts buzzed too loudly. She made a beeline for the back archives, the part of the bookshop most customers never saw. A creaky half-door marked with a handwritten sign read: "Authorized Personnel Only (which probably means YOU if you're curious enough)."

The room beyond smelled like old timber and secrets. Wooden file cabinets lined the walls, stuffed with maps, deeds, blueprints, and an assortment of Tumblebrook's obscure historical ephemera—the kind of documents most people forgot existed. Clara hadn't.

She shut the door behind her and took a seat at the worn oak table in the center of the room. From her bag, she retrieved a copy of the most recent land deed for the Tumblebrook Inn, along with a handful of older ones she'd pulled from the archives the week before. Something had been bothering her since she and Amelia found that altered map on the ridge. The property boundaries didn't match.

Clara pulled a magnifying glass from her coat pocket and leaned over the oldest document—a yellowed deed dating back to 1912. It was hand-drawn and formal, the borders of the property clearly marked with inked notations and careful script. It included the ridge —the very stretch where they'd found Vincent's boot print.

She traced the border with her fingertip, then turned to the most recent version, dated two years ago. It was digitized and sterile. The ridge wasn't included.

"That doesn't make sense," she murmured.

She reached for the registry binder—a leather-bound tome Mr. Lark maintained with obsessive care—and flipped to the index of removed or updated deeds. Her eyes skimmed the pages until she found it:

Entry 3489-B: Deed to Ridge Parcel 4C. Removed from public archives as of April 14. Note: relocated for restoration and preservation purposes.

April 14. Just a week before the Garden Festival began.

Clara narrowed her eyes.

She returned to the filing cabinet labeled "Ridge Parcels." It was meticulously organized—but one folder was missing.

"Someone took it," she whispered.

She pulled out the adjacent folders, flipping through them rapidly. No misfiles. No loose sheets. It had been removed deliberately.

Clara stood abruptly and marched back to the main shop. Mr. Lark sat at the front counter, half-hidden behind a thick copy of *The Botany of Northern Minnesota*, his glasses low on his nose.

"Mr. Lark," she said, approaching quickly. "Do you remember who accessed the ridge parcel files last?"

He blinked, clearly surfacing from a deep mental fog. "The ridge parcels? Hmm. Yes, there was someone. Gentleman, tall. New to town. Terrible tie."

"Vincent Pike?"

"That's the one. Charming, but oddly inquisitive about the land bordering the inn. Said he was working on freelance historical mapping."

Clara frowned. "Did he check anything out?"

"He said he was only referencing. But now that you mention it, he spent quite some time alone in the archive room. You don't think he—"

"I think he did more than reference," Clara said grimly.

She returned to the archive and stared at the empty space on the shelf. Vincent hadn't just browsed—he'd stolen proof. Something in that missing deed tied into his growing interest in the inn. And it likely had everything to do with the altered permit.

She jotted down the dates and cross-referenced them with her notes from the forged festival permit. The pattern was undeniable. Vincent hadn't stumbled onto an opportunity—he'd created one.

And with Lady Grey still missing, Clara feared what else he might be capable of.

Her phone buzzed. A message from Amelia: *Come to the garden room. I found something.*

Clara grabbed her bag and hurried out. When she arrived at the Tumblebrook Inn's garden room, Amelia stood beside the old chestnut hutch with a stack of papers in hand.

"Look at this," Amelia said, handing over the top sheet. "An early survey from 1934. It marks the ridge as a protected migratory bird corridor. There's even an official seal from the Minnesota Environmental Authority."

Clara's eyes widened. "That section was removed from the 2019 map. If the land's protected, any development would require extensive permits. Too much red tape for someone looking to move fast."

"Which makes the land adjacent to the inn even more valuable," Amelia said.

Clara paced. "If Vincent's consolidating land for development, the ridge is the keystone. The missing deed, the forged permit, even the catnapping—it's all about this property."

Amelia nodded. "Lady Grey must've seen something. Maybe wandered too close to whatever he's hiding."

They stood in silence as the implications settled. Clara spread out her notes.

"We need a timeline. When the deeds changed. When Vincent arrived. When the permits were issued."

Together, they built a rough chronology:

- April 1: Vincent rents the Hastings house.
- April 5: festival permit forged.
- April 14: deed disappears.
- April 18: festival begins - Lady Grey vanishes.

Clara tapped the page. "He orchestrated it. Every piece. Carefully."

Amelia's voice was low. "He's not a friendly newcomer. He's planning a takeover. And my inn is in the way."

Later that evening, Clara returned to Gossamer Fables. She scanned Mr. Lark's guest log.

April 14. Vincent Pike. Two hours logged in the archive.

She turned the page. Below, in a different hand, was a scribbled note:

Check the greenhouse blueprints.

Clara recognized the writing immediately. "Ezra."

She bolted for the edge of town. Ezra's cabin sat tucked behind wild hedges and tangled gardens. The scent of linseed oil greeted her at the door.

"I wondered when you'd come," Ezra said, opening the door with a crooked smile.

"I need the greenhouse blueprints."

He didn't question her. Just shuffled back into his cluttered studio. After a few minutes of rummaging, he produced a worn leather tube.

"These are the originals," he said. "Melvin used them when he rebuilt the greenhouse in the '90s. But they're older than that."

Clara unrolled the blueprints onto the nearest surface. Her breath caught.

There—behind the greenhouse—a tunnel. Clearly marked. Reinforced. Leading beneath the structure and toward the orchard.

"Why would there be a tunnel under a greenhouse?" she asked.

Ezra shrugged. "Old towns hide old secrets. Some say it was for bootlegging. Others think it predates that—mining, maybe."

Clara bent closer. The tunnel was labeled in faded script: *To Storage Vault B. Access limited.*

A chill crept up her spine.

"Storage of what?" she whispered.

Ezra didn't answer. Instead, he reached into his pocket and handed her a key. Brass. Ornate. Worn.

"It was tucked into the blueprint tube. Figured it might matter. Be careful down there. Things buried tend to stay buried for a reason."

Clara turned the key over in her hand. Heavy. Cold.

The conspiracy wasn't just rooted in history.

It was buried beneath it.

Chapter 18

Festival Finale

The last day of the Tumblebrook Garden Festival dawned with a sky so clear it looked painted on, not a single cloud daring to intrude. A breeze carried the perfume of lilacs, tulips, and early summer roses across town, mingled with the sugary tang of lemonade and the faint rustle of tissue paper as flower stalls unfurled. The entire village shimmered with energy that felt equal parts celebratory and expectant. It was the kind of day Amelia Farnsworth would normally savor with every fiber of her innkeeper's soul.

But not this year.

Amelia stood on the front steps of the Tumblebrook Inn in a crisp floral sundress, her auburn hair pinned neatly into a chignon that was more perfunctory than festive. Her smile, graceful as ever, was brittle. She clutched a clipboard to her chest, not because she had anything to check off—but because it kept her hands from shaking.

Festivalgoers wandered past in cheerful groups, their arms full of potted herbs, woven baskets, mason jar bouquets, and commemorative tote bags that read: "Tumblebrook Blooms!" But Amelia's attention wasn't on the guests. It was on the subtle currents moving beneath the festival's polished surface.

Behind her, the inn bustled with energy. The breakfast rush had given way to midmorning teas, and Clara was out front under a parasol, handing out rhubarb tartlets and iced hibiscus punch. The lawn had been transformed into a miniature garden paradise—canopies draped with bunting, trellises bursting with climbing vines, even a small fountain borrowed from Doris Finch's café garden.

But the usual joy was dampened by the knowledge simmering behind Amelia's eyes. The last twenty-four hours had brought a flood of revelations: Clara's discovery of the missing deed, the boundary discrepancies near the ridge, the archive record noting its suspicious removal—and Vincent Pike.

Her new neighbor, all smiles and handshakes, had been too interested in the land. Too smooth. Too calculating. And now it was clear he hadn't come to Tumblebrook for the scenery.

And Lady Grey was still gone.

The thought twisted in Amelia's chest like a thorn. Her cat had been a constant presence, an anchor in her otherwise shifting world. The garden festival was supposed to be a celebration of color and community. Instead, it had become a veneer stretched tightly over something rotten.

Amelia crossed the courtyard and moved through the crowd, pausing to wave at longtime guests and festival judges. Her outward demeanor remained calm, but her thoughts moved at double speed. Every encounter she made, every comment she heard, became another data point.

Then, by the art tent, she saw something that made her blood run cold.

Vincent Pike stood beside the community display of local watercolor paintings, chatting with none other than Margery Holmgren—the town's acting planner. Amelia had always found Margery slightly aloof but competent. Today, however, she looked tense, her lips pressed into a thin line.

Vincent leaned in, said something inaudible, and handed Margery a rectangular object. It was small and neatly wrapped in plain brown paper—an unassuming parcel.

Margery accepted it quickly and tucked it under her arm.

It was subtle. Polite. Innocuous to the untrained eye.

But Amelia saw it. The glance Vincent threw over his shoulder was anything but casual. It was practiced. Measured.

She turned on her heel and headed straight to Clara, who was now organizing pie samples on a side table next to the gazebo.

"He just handed her something," Amelia murmured, lowering her voice. "Vincent. To Margery. Near the art tent. Brown paper. I think it's a package."

Clara barely paused in slicing a tart. "That's our cue. Stay visible. Let me investigate."

With a smooth pivot, Clara set her tray down and began to meander toward the art tent, all while appearing to peruse herbs for sale. Amelia resumed her hostess duties with new sharpness, but her eyes never strayed far from Vincent. He was now at the refreshment stand, laughing with a pair of tourists as he sipped from a paper cup.

Fifteen minutes later, Clara returned, her expression tight.

"It's in her briefcase," she said quietly. "Margery slipped it inside, then locked the clasp. She hasn't let it out of her sight."

Amelia frowned. "What do you think it is?"

"Proof," Clara said. "The missing deed, maybe. Or a contract. Whatever it is, it's tied to the ridge."

Amelia glanced toward the community tent, where Margery had taken a seat beside a makeshift podium for the closing ceremony.

"We need that briefcase," she said.

Clara quirked an eyebrow. "You mean borrow it? During the festival finale?"

"Temporarily," Amelia replied. "I have a plan."

And like any good plan, it required the most dramatic man in town.

Melvin.

Melvin the gardener, who spoke to his plants, who misted begonias by moonlight, who insisted roses bloomed best when serenaded with jazz. If anyone could cause a distraction large enough to divert the crowd's attention, it was him.

Amelia approached him near the topiary contest and explained the situation in coded terms. Melvin, thrilled to be involved, insisted on wearing a cape.

"The flora shall rise," he whispered dramatically.

The closing ceremony was set for four o'clock, with the mayor slated to give his traditional speech. The entire town would be watching.

Perfect.

As the crowd gathered, Amelia loitered near the podium. Margery placed her briefcase on the ground behind her seat. Vincent stood a few paces away, arms folded, posture cool.

Then, at precisely 4:07 p.m., chaos bloomed.

"My roses!" Melvin shrieked, sprinting toward the stage with an armful of potted sunflowers, which he claimed were cross-pollinated and spiritually compromised. "The geraniums are rebelling! The sun is in retrograde!"

He tripped spectacularly over the microphone cord, sending plants flying. A cascade of petals and soil erupted across the stage, knocking over a decorative banner and nearly unseating Mayor Keegan.

The crowd gasped.

Amelia and Clara moved.

They slipped behind the podium as attention shifted entirely to Melvin's performance. Clara kept watch while Amelia knelt by the briefcase and pulled out her ring of antique inn keys.

"Come on, come on..." she whispered.

Click.

The lock popped open. Inside, beneath layers of mundane items, was a manila envelope, thick and carefully sealed.

Amelia pocketed it and re-secured the case.

By the time they returned to the inn, the festival was winding down. The scent of crushed grass and citrus hung in the air, and the sun had begun its slow descent toward the lake.

In the quiet of the back office, they opened the envelope.

Inside: a notarized land reassignment form. Parcel 4C. The ridge.

Signed by Margery. Witnessed by Vincent.

Also included was a development plan: artist renderings of modern cottages, each positioned like a scar along the ridgeline.

"They were going to bulldoze it," Clara whispered.

Amelia stared at the document. "And Lady Grey? Still missing."

At that moment, the office door creaked open.

Lady Grey, streaked with dirt and burrs, padded into the room with regal indifference. She leapt onto the desk, dropped a garden medallion from her mouth, and looked at them as if to say, What took you so long?

Amelia dropped to her knees and wrapped her arms around her cat.

"You brilliant, beautiful girl," she whispered. "You found your way home."

Clara smiled, lifting the medallion. It was from Melvin's shed— proof of where she'd been.

Together, they had the evidence.

And now, they had a choice.

Expose Vincent and Margery... or find a way to make sure justice bloomed, like everything else in Tumblebrook.

Chapter 19

From Ledger to Lies

Tumblebrook's evening light poured like amber syrup across the rooftops, casting long, golden shadows that crept slowly over cobblestone and garden paths. The town had quieted since the chaotic finale of the Garden Festival, but Clara Henderson's mind refused to follow suit. As townsfolk sipped lemonade on porches or packed up flower stands, Clara slipped into the cool dimness of Gossamer Fables with her satchel slung tightly against her shoulder.

Inside, the familiar scent of old paper and rosewood floor polish calmed her nerves. The bookshop had always been a haven. It was where she filed away more than fiction and folklore—it was where she organized truths.

She clicked on the stained-glass desk lamp in the back and pulled out the document envelope they had taken from Margery's briefcase. Inside was damning evidence, yes—but it still left gaps. They needed context. They needed motive. And above all, they needed proof that Vincent's manipulation reached deeper than a single parcel reassignment.

And that meant checking the ledgers.

Clara made her way to the back office—a tiny, overstuffed space behind a velvet curtain, half-forgotten by customers. The door creaked as she nudged it open, revealing wooden cabinets stacked high with scrolls, property registries, and receipts dating back over a hundred years.

She traced her finger along the edge of one drawer labeled "Tumblebrook Inn: 1899–Present."

With a steady breath, she pulled it open.

The ledger was there. Bound in cracked leather, thick and heavy as a fruitcake. She opened it carefully and flipped to the most recent section, scanning the entries until she hit a gap.

Pages were missing.

Her stomach twisted.

The cut was clean—someone had used a razor blade to remove at least three full sheets. She flipped backward, searching for names, references, boundaries—anything.

Parcel 4C was mentioned repeatedly in older entries. Boundary notes, inheritance from the Farnsworth family, even a hand-drawn sketch that looked suspiciously like the ridge.

The pages missing? They would've covered the last five years.

She snapped the book shut and grabbed her phone. "Amelia, we have a problem," she said as soon as the call connected.

"Missing pages?"

"How'd you know?"

"Because Margery's signature on the reassignment form dates back three years. And I only signed the annual tax documents two years ago. Something's off."

"I'm bringing the ledger. Meet me at the inn."

Ten minutes later, Clara was at the back door, the ledger tucked under one arm and her satchel bumping against her hip. Amelia let her in, looking both energized and exhausted. Lady Grey perched on the kitchen counter like a returning queen, grooming one paw with self-satisfied calm.

Clara opened the ledger on the dining room table.

"See this? This is where they sliced them out. Probably used a utility knife. Whoever did it knew exactly which pages to remove."

Amelia studied the gap. "We need to figure out what was on those pages."

"Or who had access to them," Clara said. "There's only one key to this drawer. And guess where it's supposed to be kept."

Amelia groaned. "In the bookshop desk drawer. Locked with the same key you found missing last week."

"Exactly."

Lady Grey gave a low meow and jumped down, trotting purposefully toward the sitting room.

"She knows something," Amelia said, following her. Clara trailed close behind.

The cat stopped at the fireplace, where a thin stack of old paper rested beside a forgotten folio of local poetry. Amelia crouched and carefully extracted the papers.

"Clara. Look at this."

It was one of the missing pages.

Burn marks singed the corners, but the contents were intact—an amendment notice about an easement placed on the ridge, authorized by Amelia's great-uncle in the 1960s. The easement prohibited future development.

"If this is legally binding," Clara said slowly, "Then Vincent's reassignment is null. The land can't be developed. Not without removing the easement. Which would require..."

"Public hearings. Community vote. And complete transparency," Amelia finished.

"Which they definitely didn't do."

The next morning, Clara paid a visit to Mr. Lark, the bookshop's elderly owner, who had been repairing a broken window latch upstairs during the week of the festival. He greeted her in his usual wool sweater and reading glasses, peering at her curiously.

"Did you happen to notice anyone coming in here at odd hours? Specifically near the archive cabinets?"

He frowned. "Only one, really. That young man—Vincent. Said he was researching historic garden architecture. Asked about land maps."

Clara's lips tightened. "Did he ever go near the ledger drawer?"

"I believe so. Asked me for a glass of water one day. When I returned, he was sorting through something in that area."

Clara thanked him and left quickly.

By the time she returned to the inn, her mind was buzzing.

"It's him," she said as she walked into the front parlor. "He took the pages. He planted the contract with Margery. He's been engineering this from the moment he arrived."

Amelia leaned over the counter, flipping through the salvaged ledger page. "Then it's time to go to the council. But we'll need more than a singed page and hearsay."

Clara nodded. "We'll need a witness. Someone who saw him do it. Or someone who can verify he forged that reassignment form."

Later that evening, Clara returned to Gossamer Fables, this time under the pretense of checking the poetry catalog. She wandered back to the office and began scouring old reference logs—each entry marked with the initials of the person who accessed them. In the week surrounding the missing pages, only one set of initials showed up repeatedly: V.P.

Vincent Pike had signed out three documents. Two were land use maps. The third—listed as "TBI Registry"—was the very ledger now missing pages.

They were close, close to exacting justice for Tumblebook and Amelia's family. Justice, like garden roots, always finds a way to surface.

Chapter 20

The Bumbling Officer

The morning sun filtered gently through the lace curtains of the Tumblebrook Inn's kitchen, casting delicate patterns across the polished floorboards. Amelia Farnsworth stood at the counter, her hands dusted with flour, carefully shaping lavender and lemon scones. The scent mingled with the rich aroma of fresh-brewed coffee and the faint tang of rosemary from the planter on the sill. Lady Grey, now restored to her full feline dignity after her recent adventure, dozed contentedly on the windowsill, her gray fur warm from the sun. To Amelia, it felt like the calm before a storm.

She was just about to call Clara down when a screech of brakes shattered the quiet. A moment later, someone knocked at the front door with unmistakable urgency.

Clara, descending the staircase at her usual brisk pace, exchanged a look with Amelia. "Expecting anyone?"

"Not unless someone woke up desperate for scones," Amelia replied, wiping her hands on her apron.

She opened the door to reveal Officer Theodore Wexley—Tumblebrook's well-meaning but hopelessly bumbling policeman.

His uniform was slightly askew, one bootlace untied, and he clutched a manila folder as if it might vanish if he let go.

"Morning, Ms. Farnsworth! Ms. Henderson! Fortunate timing, truly!" he exclaimed, out of breath despite the short walk from his car.

"Come in, Officer," Amelia said. "Everything alright?"

"Yes—well, no—well, that is... I was sorting mail at the station. Bit of a mess after the festival. And would you believe what I found in Grady's mailbox?" He waved the folder dramatically.

"Grady the butcher?" Clara asked.

"The very same! But this wasn't about meat. No, this," he said, laying the folder on the counter, "is a set of land rezoning forms. And your name is on them, Ms. Farnsworth. Along with some other rather interesting ones."

Clara opened the folder immediately, eyes scanning the documents. Amelia leaned over her shoulder.

The forms were polished and precise. Amelia's name was listed on a proposed land reassignment. But what made her chest tighten was another name—Vincent Pike.

"These were filed four months ago," Amelia said, her voice tightening. "Linked to commercial development. Dependent on the successful completion of the Garden Festival. This is before any of our recent discoveries."

"And the ridge?" Clara pointed to the highlighted boundary line. "That's Parcel 4C. The same disputed land from the missing deed."

"We never authorized this," Amelia added.

Lady Grey leapt down from the windowsill and strode over to the counter, hopping up beside the folder and giving it a long, appraising sniff before settling on top of it, her tail twitching with disdain.

"You did the right thing bringing this to us," Clara said to Wexley.

He beamed. "Well, I was just trying to find my lunch. Thought I left it near the post bins. Grady's box is right next to mine. This caught my eye—the font didn't exactly scream 'butcher invoice,' you know?"

Amelia chuckled softly. "Even your clumsiness has its moments."

"Always happy to help!" Wexley said proudly.

Clara flipped through the forms again. "Look here—the notary seal is misaligned. It's printed, not embossed. And the signature is clearly forged."

"So, it's fake," Amelia confirmed.

"Sloppy forgery. But enough to slide by unnoticed."

They all paused.

"Officer," Clara said carefully. "If you find anything else out of place, could you quietly pass it along to us?"

Wexley straightened. "A confidential courier. Consider it handled."

Amelia smiled. "With scones and coffee in perpetuity."

That afternoon, they brought the documents to Miss Eliza Burbridge, the town notary. Her ivy-covered office behind Town Hall smelled of lemon oil and tidy order. Eliza examined the forms through a magnifying glass.

"These never crossed my desk," she said crisply. "And this seal hasn't been used in five years. Whoever forged this had access to old template forms."

"Vincent's firm has ties to historic preservation," Amelia said slowly. "He could've accessed archived zoning documents."

"Then it's premeditated," Clara concluded.

Back at the inn, the parlor became their war room. Notes were pinned across the mantel. Lady Grey supervised from her perch.

"He's been planning this for months," Clara said. "Charm, lies, false paperwork. He knew exactly what he was doing."

"And he counted on us not noticing," Amelia added.

The next morning, Amelia met Mayor Keegan with a full portfolio: Eliza's affidavit, the forged forms, and a timeline of Vincent's actions.

The mayor listened with grim silence, then gave a slow, heavy sigh. "You understand what you're suggesting? If this is true, it's not just a scandal. It's fraud."

"I know," Clara said. "But we can't let them tear up that ridge. Not for some luxury development."

"This is enough to convene the council," he said. "I'll issue a special summons. Quietly."

That evening, the town council gathered in the smaller chamber of Town Hall.

Clara, Amelia, and Eliza entered armed with a box of evidence—and a cat who refused to stay behind.

Lady Grey sat smugly in Amelia's tote bag, poking her head out as if to offer commentary. Officer Wexley even testified to the unusual mail mix-up. When Eliza confirmed the forgery under oath, murmurs echoed through the room.

Then, to everyone's surprise, Margery Holmgren stood.

"I was misled," she said. "Vincent promised revitalization. I didn't realize the ridge had an easement. He said it had expired. I'm sorry."

Amelia looked at her—firm, but calm. "You can still help make it right."

Vincent Pike would be held accountable.

Lady Grey purred, pleased. Justice had a scent—and she was on the trail.

Chapter 21

Into the Crawlspace

Darkness clung to the edges of the crawlspace like a second skin. The air was thick with mildew, dust, and something cloyingly sweet—like old apples left to rot in the sun. Lady Grey crouched low beneath the floorboards of an abandoned gardener's cottage on the outskirts of Tumblebrook. Her wiry body, hidden beneath plush, silver fur, moved with practiced stillness. Each breath came measured and alert, her amber eyes gleaming with purpose.

She had escaped her captors days ago—though time, for her, passed not in hours but in scent shifts and shadow turns. Her coat was dulled by grime and burrs, but something inside her had sharpened. A primal resolve surged beneath the velvet exterior. She was no one's housecat now. She was a sentinel with silent paws.

The escape had been perilous: a loosened plank, a downpour softening the wood, and a thunderstorm that masked her desperate scrabbling. She had clawed, twisted, and wriggled through splinters. Her tail had snagged on a rusty nail. But when she burst into the open night, the air had tasted like freedom.

Following faint traces of earth, moss, and fertilizer—Melvin the gardener's unmistakable trail—she'd arrived here, beneath the bones of a long-forgotten cottage. Once nourished, once whole again, she'd returned to investigate. There was something she had missed in the chaos of escape.

Inside the crawlspace, thin shafts of moonlight pierced cracks in the slats, illuminating what looked like fallen leaves—but they were pages. Dozens of them. Water-stained, dog-eared, heavily annotated. Some contained diagrams. Others bore looping handwriting in dark ink. But all shared one scent: Vincent Pike.

Lady Grey moved among them like mist over morning dew. Her tail twitched as she scanned the clutter, each page whispering its own silent story. One rustled beneath her paw—stirred by a passing breeze. She sat back and nosed it forward. It was a boundary map—of the Tumblebrook Inn's property. Heavy black lines re-drew the gardens. A thick circle surrounded the tulip beds. A bold X slashed across the ridge.

She went still.

This was no garden shed.

This was Vincent's staging ground. A lair, built on deception.

Above, the cottage groaned under the weight of silence. A flowerpot rolled. A wheelbarrow rusted in the tall grass. The world had forgotten this place. But Vincent had not.

Lady Grey scratched a diagonal mark into a wooden beam—her signature. Then she swatted one annotated page toward a wall opening. The wind caught it and whisked it into the night, where it landed near a lichen-covered stone at the treeline.

The same spot Clara had passed. The same one Amelia had noted weeks ago.

Coincidence was for humans. Lady Grey trusted instinct.

She crept deeper into the crawlspace.

At its far edge, hidden behind a slumped support beam, sat a cracked crate. She sniffed once, then pounced. The brittle lid gave way with a snap. Inside lay more evidence: festival permits, zoning maps, and a letter addressed to E.B.—Eliza Burbridge. Lady Grey pressed her nose to the parchment.

She knew that scent.

A torn postscript peeked out: Burn after the festival.

She growled low in her throat.

Beneath the paperwork lay a black-and-white photograph of the inn before its expansion. A red circle marked a now-demolished tool-shed—once positioned at the end of the wildflower path. Now Amelia's tulip bed.

Why mark a vanished structure unless something buried beneath it still mattered?

She investigated further. The wall to the west smelled of ash and lavender. She pawed carefully, dislodging a warped plank. Ash drifted like brittle snow. Beneath it, a scorched notebook lay half-preserved. Most of its pages had turned to dust—but one remained.

It bore a hand-drawn sigil—identical to the watermark from the ransom note.

Lady Grey's breath quickened. She gripped the page between her teeth.

This wasn't just revenge now. Or fear.

Someone had tried to force Amelia's hand. The catnapping hadn't been mere leverage—it had been a calculated move in a far-reaching land grab.

She emerged from the crawlspace, wet leaves clinging to her coat. Above, clouds were gathering. Thunder echoed in the distance. The world had shifted.

She darted into the trees.

* * *

At the inn, Amelia and Clara paced the library, documents and blueprints strewn across the table. Earlier that morning, Lady Grey slipped away from the safety of the Inn, almost unnoticed. Except by Amelia.

"We're missing something," Clara muttered. "There's a blank spot between the forged records and the development map."

"Lady Grey's out there," Amelia said quietly. "And I think she's looking too."

* * *

Back at the treeline, the wind picked up. Lady Grey padded steadily toward home, her tail high.

This time, she wouldn't just return.

She'd lead them to the truth.

Chapter 22

Blueprints and Butterflies

The scent of old paper and musty wood filled Clara's nostrils the moment she stepped into the bookshop's attic. Dust swirled in the thin beams of light slicing through a cracked windowpane. She brushed her sleeve against a sagging shelf and sneezed.

"Bless you," Mr. Lark called faintly from the foot of the stairs, his voice muffled behind a copy of *Rare Cartographies of the North Shore*.

Clara smiled wryly and turned back to the chest in front of her. It groaned as she eased open the lid, revealing a mishmash of rolled maps, brittle folders, and ledger books. She was looking for anything that might connect the recent property discrepancies to a larger scheme—and the attic was her last hope.

She unrolled a large blueprint, its edges frayed with age. The paper was thin and yellowed. Her eyes scanned the familiar outlines of Tumblebrook, searching for something—anything—unusual.

And there it was.

In the lower left corner, nearly faded with time, was an insignia she immediately recognized. A butterfly.

Not just any butterfly.

A double-winged silhouette surrounded by an ornate compass rose. The unmistakable emblem of the Monarch Society.

Clara's breath hitched. Yet another link to the historical collective that once wielded significant influence in Tumblebrook—wealthy families who had documented and claimed large swaths of land under the guise of heritage preservation.

This particular blueprint bore the words *Monarch Society Surveyor Authority, Est. 1884* beneath the symbol. It confirmed her suspicion: someone was reviving old claims through these historic documents, possibly to justify a hostile rezoning of property.

She gently lifted several more blueprints from the chest. Each one contained additions and annotations not found in the town's modern survey records—tiny structures, unknown property lines, and underground passageways. One appeared to map the ridge where she and Amelia had discovered the underground chamber. Another showed penciled-in symbols near Melvin's greenhouse.

Her fingers tingled as she traced the winding lines. Whoever had drawn these plans was mapping out a hidden network of influence, buried beneath the flowers and history of the Garden Festival. She could practically feel the web tightening.

Tucked among the blueprints was a crumbling leather-bound journal. Clara flipped through its pages with cautious reverence. The entries, dated over a century ago, documented the Monarch Society's land dealings. One name kept recurring: E. Burbridge. She frowned. A familiar name—possibly a relative of Eliza Burbridge, the town councilwoman.

In the back pages, she found a folded sheet with hand-rendered schematics of ritual gardens—grids and flower plots marked not for aesthetics, but for signaling. Marginal notes read: *Markers for memory access* and *Entrances masked beneath bloom.*

Clara jotted a few observations into her notepad, thoughts racing. She needed more context.

She clutched the blueprint and rushed down the stairs, startling Mr. Lark, who nearly dropped his book.

"Clara!" he exclaimed, flailing slightly. "What on earth?"

"Look at this," she said, spreading the blueprint across the nearest counter.

Mr. Lark blinked behind his spectacles. "My word, more blueprints from the Monarch Society? You know, they used to be on the plaques near the old town hall. They were like a secret council at one point."

"Did they actually survey land?" Clara asked.

"Oh yes," Mr. Lark said, leaning closer. "They had their own engineers, even a charter. Claimed they were preserving Tumblebrook's legacy. But people whispered they were consolidating power. A lot of their records vanished after the Great Fire of '47."

Clara's jaw tightened. "Or were hidden intentionally."

Mr. Lark nodded slowly. "Quite possibly. Some say their descendants still pull strings behind the scenes."

She pointed at a marginal note scribbled in faded ink: *Verify with Burbridge vault.* Her stomach dropped.

"Burbridge," she murmured. "It keeps coming back to her."

Back at the Tumblebrook Inn, Clara spread the documents across the sitting room table. Amelia sat opposite her, a mug of mint tea in her hands.

Clara tapped the corner of the blueprint. "Multiple maps show structures and boundaries that don't align with current zoning. And look at this—plans for what looks like a cellar or chamber under the tulip garden."

Amelia studied the sketch. "This must be the same chamber where we discovered Annie's Monarch Society involvement."

Clara nodded. "It's all connected. And with their involvement, this isn't just about one greedy developer. It's a network—possibly old money—trying to resurrect a claim that was never legally valid."

Amelia tapped her mug. "So someone is forging a new land map under the guise of restoring historic boundaries."

"Exactly. And they're using old festival permits and misfiled deeds to do it. The Monarch Society might be the key to unraveling who benefits most from the rezoning."

Lady Grey leapt onto the windowsill, fresh from her latest mission, her amber eyes narrowing at something outside. She let out a low trill, tail swishing.

Clara followed her gaze. Across the street, a figure ducked around the corner of the bookstore, too quickly to identify. Her pulse quickened.

"They're watching us now," she said.

Amelia rose. "Then we need to move faster than they do."

They both leaned over the table. A single sheet fluttered in the breeze from the open window, landing near Lady Grey, who blinked slowly and pawed it into place.

The blueprint showed the hidden chamber they were in stretched beneath the tulip garden.

Clara gasped. "That's it. That's what they're after."

Amelia narrowed her eyes. "Then that's where we go next."

They spent the next hour cross-referencing the blueprint with a recent town zoning map, marking off inconsistencies. Clara highlighted several areas around the tulip garden, Melvin's greenhouse, and parts of the inn's backyard—sections aligning closely with old Monarch Society annotations.

As they worked, dusk fell and the inn grew quiet. Outside, wind rattled the flower boxes on the porch rail. The sense of being watched did not fade.

Clara flipped to the back of the Monarch ledger and found a tucked-in envelope addressed in elegant script: *To the Custodian of Memory*. Inside was a single page describing a ritual garden design meant to mask subterranean entrances. A garden where specific flower beds signaled where not to dig.

She handed it to Amelia, who read with wide eyes.

"This isn't just about land," Amelia whispered. "It's about keeping secrets buried."

And for the first time since Lady Grey vanished, both women felt the truth might be far more dangerous—and older—than either of them had imagined.

Chapter 23

Whispers at the Window

The lake shimmered beneath the morning sun, calm and mirror-like, reflecting the tall reeds that flanked its banks. Amelia Farnsworth stood at the edge of the Tumblebrook Inn's dock with a watering can in hand, watching the slow ripple of water move lazily toward the far shore. It should have been peaceful—comforting, even. But there was something in the air today. A prickling on the back of her neck. An echo of something unseen, but very much present.

She placed the watering can beside a flowerpot and adjusted the brim of her straw hat. The garden festival had come to a close, and although the guests were thinning out, the residue of celebration clung to the town like flower petals stuck to damp cobblestones. Yet under all the festivity, unease festered.

Lady Grey was back, again—but her reappearance had done little to quell the overarching mystery. If anything, it had only added more questions. Her collar had been missing, and the small garden medallion found near Melvin's toolshed remained unexplained. Clara's discovery of the Monarch Society's blueprints continued to unfurl in layers Amelia barely understood. And the inn—her beloved inn—felt like it was holding its breath.

And now this.

Amelia lifted her gaze to the opposite side of the lake, where the land rose in a gentle slope, dense with birch and pine. Someone was there.

A silhouette—tall, unmoving—half-obscured by the trees.

She blinked, adjusting her stance. For a moment, the figure remained still. Then, like a phantom, it slipped behind a tree and vanished.

Her stomach tightened. "No more shadows," she muttered, brushing off her hands. But her feet had already decided. She moved forward—not running, but with the urgent purpose of someone who'd had quite enough of mystery.

She passed through the inn's rear gate, taking the old footpath that curved around the lake. The trail was narrow and half-hidden by underbrush. Birds chirped overhead, oblivious to her tension. As she walked, a squirrel darted across her boots and she jumped, letting out a small gasp before chuckling at herself. "Get a grip, Farnsworth."

The trees thickened as she approached the lake's far side. The light filtered differently here—cooler, less golden. It cast long fingers of shadow along moss-covered rocks and created the illusion of movement in the corners of her eyes. She paused near the boulder where Lady Grey's claw marks had once been discovered, scanning the trees.

"Hello?" she called, her voice steady. "I saw you."

Nothing.

Only the soft rustle of leaves and the gentle lap of water against the shore.

She stepped farther in, where a game trail twisted uphill. Boot prints. Fresh. A size or two larger than hers, patterned with deep tread—different from Melvin's gardening clogs or Clara's soft-soled flats. These were hiking boots, and the angle of the prints suggested a male gait.

The prints led her through a shallow ravine, where the lake came into partial view again. The earth was soft and springy from last week's rain. She bent down, examining the tread. Not deep enough for a heavy man. Average build. Possibly Vincent Pike?

She followed the trail as it curved to the right and found herself at a clearing—a shallow rise overlooking the lake. Empty. No person. Just silence. The air was unnervingly still.

But there—by the base of a tree—something glinted.

Amelia crouched and picked it up. A brass button. Not modern. Worn, possibly vintage. It bore a delicate etching of a butterfly surrounded by a starburst.

Her breath caught. "Monarch Society," she whispered.

Was this a signal? A message left behind? Or had she startled someone before they could finish what they'd intended?

As she rose, she turned slowly in place, scanning the edges of the clearing. Broken branches. A scrap of fabric—a torn bit of wool—snagged on a twig. The same deep navy hue Vincent had worn two nights ago.

She took out her phone and snapped photos of the button and the trail before pocketing the artifact. Her mind buzzed. Had Vincent been here? Had he dropped the button, or was someone else involved?

As she turned to go, a soft creak caught her ear. She froze. From just beyond the clearing, where the path narrowed into a natural corridor of trees, came the sound of retreating footsteps—slow and deliberate, crunching leaves beneath cautious strides.

She rushed toward the sound, but by the time she reached the corridor, it was empty. No footprints. No sign of movement. Just a stillness so heavy it made her skin crawl.

She lingered for several minutes, listening. Then, reluctantly, turned back toward the inn.

The walk back felt longer. Her adrenaline had drained, leaving her tense and thoughtful. At the back door, she slipped in and found Clara at the parlor table, frowning over one of the attic blueprints.

Clara looked up. "Where did you go? I was about to send a search party."

Amelia hesitated. "I saw someone. Across the lake. I went to find them—this was left behind."

She placed the brass button on the table.

Clara picked it up, turning it over. "Same insignia. These aren't common. Someone wanted you to find this."

"Or they dropped it by accident," Amelia said, though her tone lacked conviction.

Lady Grey hopped onto the table, sniffed the button, then let out a low, disgruntled meow.

"She doesn't like it either," Amelia said softly.

They sat in silence for a moment before Clara opened a drawer and pulled out a folder labeled *Historical Correspondence*. Inside were old letters, land records, and scanned photos from Tumblebrook's earliest days. She laid out one document in particular—a faded, hand-drawn town map with several buildings circled in red ink.

"These belonged to known members of the Monarch Society in the 1800s," Clara explained. "And this clearing—right where you found the button—was once a meeting spot, according to this letter from the librarian's archives."

"So whoever was watching me knew exactly where they were standing," Amelia said.

Clara nodded. "And they wanted you to know it."

Amelia paced in front of the fireplace, heart still racing. She thought back on recent events—the forged permit, Vincent's vague threats, the missing deed pages. Everything was circling the Monarch Society. But why now? What had changed?

Lady Grey leapt from the table and padded toward the front window, ears twitching.

Amelia followed her gaze. Across the street, a car she didn't recognize sat idling, the driver hidden behind a reflective windshield. It lingered for a moment longer, then drove off slowly.

Clara joined her. "We're being watched. Not just today. Probably all week."

"And not just by one person," Amelia said.

She straightened. "It's time we stop reacting," she said. "And start pushing back."

Clara met her eyes, full of resolve. "Then let's find out exactly what the Monarch Society buried—and why someone still wants it hidden."

Lady Grey gave a chirp of agreement, her amber eyes sharp as she curled into a chair near the fire.

Outside, clouds gathered over the lake, a slow-moving storm rolling in from the north.

Chapter 24

Talks with Mr. Lark

Tumblebrook's morning hush was broken only by the rhythmic tapping of Clara Henderson's shoes against the cobblestone path leading to Gossamer Fables. The bookstore, nestled between the apothecary and the milliner's shop, looked as though it had been carved from a forgotten century. Wooden shutters flanked tall windows, and a hand-painted sign above the door swung gently in the breeze. Inside, the scent of paper and pine polish swirled through the air—a perfume Clara found both calming and invigorating.

She arrived before the shop officially opened, but Mr. Lark had already turned the front sign to read "Come In, If You Must." Clara smiled. She unlocked the side entrance, set her bag behind the counter, and made her way to the back reading room. Mr. Lark sat there, surrounded by a fortress of books, peering over a pair of half-moon spectacles.

"Clara," he said without looking up, "I thought you might come early. The tea's already steeped. Darjeeling. Strong."

She sank into the opposite chair, grateful for both the tea and his intuition. "I need to talk to you about the inn's land records," she began. "And something you mentioned a few months ago—about the founding families."

Mr. Lark folded the corner of his page and removed his glasses. "The Monarch Society?"

Clara blinked. "What else can you tell me about them?"

"They're like an old book club that decided democracy was too slow." He poured her a cup of tea. "But you're looking for more than spooky stories. So, what's happened?"

Clara pulled the blueprint from her satchel—the one bearing the butterfly insignia. Mr. Lark's brow arched.

"Found in the bookshop attic," she said. "But I think there's more in the archives. Possibly in the locked cabinet upstairs."

Mr. Lark nodded and rose, heading for the stairs. Clara followed, her heart pounding. The top floor was dim and musty, lined with locked cabinets and forgotten ledgers. From a ring of brass keys, Mr. Lark selected one and turned it in the oldest cabinet's lock. The door creaked open to reveal boxes marked PRIVATE ESTATE CORRE-SPONDENCE. He handed her a faded journal with a cracked leather spine.

"This belonged to Edwin Ashcroft. Founder of the Tumblebrook Inn."

Clara's fingers trembled as she opened the journal. Inside were notes about construction, seasonal flooding, tenant squabbles—and tucked between pages, letters. Letters to and from Nathaniel Pike.

"Vincent Pike's ancestor," Clara said aloud.

Mr. Lark leaned closer. "Those two were friends. Until they weren't."

The letters outlined a falling out—land lines, ownership rights, and a contested parcel where the inn's gardens now flourished. One entry in Ashcroft's journal read:

The south ridge boundary is firm. No matter what Nathaniel claims, I've the original deed.

"But we haven't found that deed," Clara murmured.

"Because it was removed," Mr. Lark said gravely. "Not lost—erased."

Clara scanned a second letter. Nathaniel had written in frustration:

If I cannot secure the land through law, I will secure it through legacy.

A chill slid down Clara's spine. "Do you think Vincent is continuing that plan?"

Mr. Lark looked out the small attic window toward the inn in the distance. "I think legacies in this town rarely die. They just shift into shadow."

They spent the next hour cataloging every document referencing Ashcroft, Pike, and the southern boundary. Mr. Lark dictated notes while Clara transcribed, the past bleeding into the present with each curl of ink. One page bore a sketched diagram. Clara recognized it instantly—the garden boulder. Underneath it, a crude "X." Beside it: *Storage for Society instruments.*

"There's something buried under that boulder," Clara whispered.

Mr. Lark nodded solemnly. "And someone doesn't want it found."

Clara packed the journal into her satchel and thanked him. As she turned to leave, Mr. Lark called out, "Wait. There's more. Follow me."

He led her through the back hallway into a small annex room, where a tall glass case stood draped in a faded velvet cloth. With a reverent gesture, he pulled the cloth away, revealing an intricately etched map beneath the glass.

"This is one of the oldest renderings of Tumblebrook's founding plots," he said. "It was commissioned by Ashcroft himself—and it shows something strange."

He pointed to a peculiar symbol not found on any modern maps —a looping butterfly inked in pale gold.

"That's not decorative," he said. "It marks Monarch jurisdiction. And it's planted right on top of the ridge that borders your garden."

Clara leaned closer, eyes wide. "How long have you known this existed?"

"Years," Mr. Lark said with a sigh. "But no one ever took it seriously. Most thought it part of the inn's local lore. But you and Amelia are the first in decades to chase the truth."

Clara spent another hour poring over ledgers, maps, and documents. Hidden among them was a faded inventory sheet marked: *Monarch Holdings – Relic Transfers*. Among the items listed were brass tokens, ceremonial medallions, and a set of keys marked *Cottage 12 – Root Cellar Access*.

Clara froze. The same cottage where Lady Grey had been spotted.

"Mr. Lark, do you think the Monarch Society is still active?"

He didn't answer immediately. Instead, he walked to the window and stared out at the town square, remembering the final day of the Garden Festival. "I think some secrets bury themselves until someone's bold enough to dig them up. And I think you're holding the right shovel."

As Clara prepared to leave, she spotted a bound leather ledger left on a side table. Inside were handwritten codes resembling ciphers she had seen in the margins of Tobias Greer's travel journal—the same ones referencing secret locations around the lake and inn.

"This connects to Tobias," she murmured.

Mr. Lark turned sharply. "Tobias Greer was researching the Monarch Society. He left notes hidden in books here—notes I've never found. Until now."

Clara took a final look around the room, her heart racing. She felt the weight of truth settling across her shoulders. Everything was converging: Tobias's disappearance, Vincent's motives, and the land that might hold more than just flowers and secrets.

She stepped outside into a sky streaked with gray. The wind carried the scent of fresh earth and a storm on the horizon. Tumblebrook no longer felt quite so quaint—it felt like a story just beginning to unfold.

Chapter 25

Clawed Message

Lady Grey awoke in the dim hush beneath the floorboards of the abandoned cottage, her amber eyes catching the faintest glint of morning light spilling through cracks in the warped wooden slats above. Dust motes danced in the beam like fireflies, settling softly on her whiskers. For most creatures, this crawlspace would feel suffocating —buried in shadow and stale with mildew and forgotten things—but for a cat of her temperament and cleverness, it was merely a temporary puzzle.

She had survived worse. Escaped tighter spaces. Outsmarted humans and their clumsy traps. And she wasn't done yet.

Lady Grey had ended up here two nights ago, revisiting her once-used hiding spot. She remembered a frantic dash through the thickets bordering the garden maze and a desperate leap through the shattered cottage window, she ensured her captor hadn't seen her. She followed the same path her tiny frame had once slipped through—a loose board beneath the porch offering refuge from voices and closing footsteps. What she had stumbled into was far more than shelter.

She had been drawn here not by accident but by instinct—a lingering scent, a quiet resonance she couldn't name. In her frantic pawing through the dusty floor and crumbling insulation, she had discovered something buried. Something forgotten. Something important.

Lady Grey stood, stretched her lithe frame, and sniffed the air. Beneath the musk of earth and wood, she caught it again: the metallic tang of ink, the aged spice of vellum. Someone had stashed something down here—papers, yes, and something else. A trace of beeswax? Maybe even old tobacco smoke.

She padded carefully over a mat of insulation and debris, her paws silent. One section of the floor dipped slightly under her weight. Beneath it, layers of old parchment were arranged like offerings in a forgotten shrine.

Her sharp claws extended as she swiped gently at the edge. The papers fluttered, the floor groaning with the whisper of long-held secrets. She pawed one over: a handwritten list. Names. Dates. Parcel numbers. Then another page: a delicate, embossed butterfly in midflight—the unmistakable Monarch Society seal. Another document lay pinned beneath a rusted tin, its annotations in red ink eerily familiar.

She sat back, flicking her tail. Clara had been right.

The floor creaked above—barely a shift, but enough to send her crouching into shadow. When no footsteps followed, she returned to her task. Her thoughts wandered to Amelia and Clara. Had they figured out the truth yet? Were they close?

She couldn't let these documents go unnoticed. But they were too delicate to drag through the crawlspace. Even she, magnificent though she was, couldn't carry a ledger in her teeth. She needed to leave a sign.

She turned toward the thickest patch of dust near a low beam beside the stone foundation. Using one paw, she began to scratch a message. It took patience, precision, and a lot of tail twitching.

FENCELINELIES

She stepped back and stared. It wasn't elegant, but it would do.

Any human clever enough to decode land deeds could interpret a feline communiqué.

Satisfied, she scratched once more at the floorboard, unearthing a final corner of parchment—a hand-drawn diagram with arrows pointing toward the ridge. She mewed softly. That ridge again. The one Clara and Amelia had examined. The one with the sun-bleached boulder and mismatched survey lines.

Lady Grey pawed a tuft of fur loose and batted it toward the cracked crawlspace entrance. Then, with effort, she wriggled through the narrow opening into the cool spring morning. Dew clung to the grass, dampening her coat, but the air was fresh, bright, and heavy with lilac.

She darted for the underbrush, tail high. She was going home.

At the inn, Amelia sipped tea on the wraparound porch, worry creasing her brow as she stared out at the lake. Clara sat beside her, an open journal in her lap and Mr. Lark's map spread between them.

"It all circles back to the inn," Clara said. "The blueprints, the deeds, the ridge—it's like everything Vincent's done was meant to lay claim to the land beneath our feet."

Amelia nodded. "And Lady Grey knew something. I swear she tried to show me before she vanished."

A flash of gray darted across the garden path. A blur. A meow.

Amelia bolted upright, knocking over her tea. "Lady Grey! You need to stop disappearing like that."

The cat bounded up the porch steps and leapt into her arms, half-chirping, half-purring. Clara reached to scratch behind her ears and froze.

"Wait. What's that on her paw?"

Dust clung to the fur. Dirt streaks marked her flank. Her back paws were caked in something darker—soot? Or remnants of something disturbed underground?

Amelia's heart pounded. "She came from somewhere. Somewhere important."

Lady Grey mewed again and leapt from Amelia's lap, trotting toward the ridge path as if to say: Follow me.

They did.

At the ridge, beneath old birch trees, Lady Grey stopped and looked back, tail flicking insistently.

Clara exhaled. "She wants us to go back to the cottage. Now."

The path twisted back through bramble and meadow until they reached the abandoned structure—gray, sagging, forgotten by most, but not by Lady Grey. The crawlspace yawned like an open secret. Clara slipped on gloves and ducked beneath while Amelia held back the vines.

Inside, Clara's flashlight swept over relics: splintered crates, broken jars, bundles of brittle paper stacked beneath floorboards. At the far end, she gasped.

"Here! She was here, Amelia—look!"

Amelia crouched beside her. "It's the Monarch seal. This paper's at least fifty years old. Maybe more."

"These are land records," Clara whispered. "And notes—some in the same handwriting as Tobias Greer's journal. Look—his cipher. This wasn't just a stash. It was a hideaway."

Lady Grey nosed past them, circling the spot where she'd left her message, purring with purpose.

"FENCE LINE LIES," Clara read aloud.

They turned to Lady Grey, who blinked slowly and sat, queenly in the silhouettes of light.

Amelia read aloud from one faded sheet: *Parcel K to be held under shadow claim until suitable inheritor emerges. F.L.L.*

She looked at Clara. "F.L.L.—Fence Line Lies. She didn't just write a warning. She gave us initials tied to the plan."

Clara's mind raced. "These papers prove there was an active land claim hidden from public record. If Vincent knew about it..."

"Then the entire garden festival could've been a front," Amelia said.

They bundled the documents, took photos, and returned to the inn as dusk fell. The lake glimmered under pale starlight. Somewhere out there, the Monarch Society's legacy still breathed.

Lady Grey perched on the windowsill that evening, purring as though her work was done.

But Amelia knew better.

The truth was still buried.

Just not for much longer.

Chapter 26

The Fence Test

The morning sun cast a soft golden light over the Tumblebrook Inn's garden, illuminating dew-kissed petals and the whitewashed fence that had long stood as a familiar border between Amelia's beloved property and the encroaching woodland beyond. Amelia stood on the porch, surveying the quiet scene, the chirping of sparrows a gentle contrast to the storm of thoughts swirling in her mind. The aroma of lavender from the garden beds mingled with the scent of coffee wafting from the kitchen window.

Lady Grey lay coiled at her feet, tail flicking thoughtfully, as if she too were weighing the pieces of the mystery now unfolding. The message the cat had clawed into the dust—"FENCE LINE LIES"—was no longer a poetic warning. It was a directive. And a damning one.

Clara emerged from the inn carrying a long measuring tape, a canvas bag slung over her shoulder filled with a compass, notepad, and several photocopies of the town's oldest survey maps. Her boots crunched across the flagstones, and the look on her face confirmed what Amelia already knew: today was not about curiosity. It was about proving theft—and reclaiming what had been quietly taken.

"Ready?" Clara asked, raising a brow.

Amelia nodded. "As I'll ever be. Let's find out where this truth has been buried."

They began their measurements from the northeast corner of the inn, where the original survey pin—a rusted iron spike—still jutted from the soil like a forgotten sentinel. According to the documents they'd found in the crawlspace of the abandoned cottage, the property line should run forty-eight paces southwest to the ridge.

"One... two... three..." Clara counted aloud, measuring carefully while keeping the tape taut. Lady Grey padded behind them, tail held high, her paws silent against the grass. Birds chirped overhead, and somewhere beyond the hedge maze, faint echoes of laughter and music floated on the breeze.

At thirty-five paces, they reached the white fence.

"That's thirteen paces short," Amelia murmured, the weight of the discrepancy pressing on her chest.

Clara scribbled a note in her journal. "It's not just a mistake. This was moved intentionally. Someone shortened the inn's lot."

Amelia bent to examine the fence posts. The wood was newer than she remembered—pressure-treated pine rather than the grayed cedar of the original fence.

"These boards aren't more than five years old," she said, fingers trailing over the smoother grain.

"Which lines up," Clara said, flipping to a page in her notes. "That's when the town approved the Garden Festival expansion. And guess who was on the planning committee?"

"Vincent Pike. He was nosing around here earlier than we thought."

The name left a bitter taste.

They walked along the fence line, checking angles and distances. At each corner, the measurements deviated slightly but consistently, confirming their growing suspicion: the inn's boundary had been quietly shifted, and the land absorbed into the festival grounds and, by extension, Pike's development project.

At the far end, Lady Grey darted through a break in the fence and disappeared into the underbrush.

"Lady Grey!" Amelia called, alarm tightening her voice.

But instead of returning, the cat let out a sharp, commanding meow from deeper in the woods.

"She wants us to follow," Clara said, already moving.

They followed Lady Grey down a slope veiled with creeping ferns and ivy. The air was cooler here, shaded by tall birch and oak. At the bottom, nestled between two birch trees, was a forgotten iron post—nearly identical to the original survey marker.

Clara knelt to examine it. "It's stamped. Look—1497. This is one of the original corner markers."

"Then this proves it," Amelia said. "The fence isn't on the original line. Vincent's project illegally absorbed part of the inn's land."

Clara stood, brushing off her jeans. "With the Monarch Society's old maps and this physical marker, we can expose it."

They marked the post's location with flags and took a series of photos with Amelia's phone. Then, retracing their steps, they faced the fence again—this time from the side that told the truth.

Later that afternoon, they returned to the inn's library. Maps, blueprints, and old ledgers sprawled across the table like a cartographer's battlefield. The room smelled of old books and chamomile from a forgotten cup of tea. Clara hovered over a document from the crawlspace.

"This mentions a clause about boundary reassessment... but only if all adjoining property owners agree. Amelia, did you ever sign anything like that?"

"No," Amelia said firmly. "Not in twenty years. No one's ever asked."

"Then Pike's entire acquisition was built on a lie. He forged compliance."

They sat in silence. The scale of deception was staggering. Amelia reached for her tea, now cold.

"Do you think Officer Wexley will help us? He did bring us those zoning documents."

Clara sighed. "I'm not sure. But he's our next step. Either him, or Doris. If anyone's heard whispers about Pike's deals, it's her."

Lady Grey hopped onto the table and carefully placed her paw on a corner of one particular map.

Amelia leaned closer. "She's pointing to the old tool shed near the western garden."

Clara's eyes lit up. "That was part of the original boundary line too, before the garden paths changed. We should check it."

They ventured back outside, shadows lengthening across the lawn. The shed loomed, quiet and forgotten, its door creaking as Clara pushed it open. Dust hung in the air like memory. Inside, beneath a tattered tarp, lay an old surveyor's tripod and measuring tools, each stamped with the town's seal and tagged as property of the planning office.

Clara knelt and pulled out a folded document wedged beneath the equipment.

"This is a field sketch," she whispered. "Dated three years ago. It shows the old fence line... and someone's handwritten note: 'Shift 15 feet—discreetly.'"

Amelia took a shaky breath. "We need to show this to the town council. They need to see how deep this goes."

Clara nodded. "And if they won't listen, we go public. We'll bring the whole truth into the light."

Back at the inn, Clara spent the evening assembling a comprehensive file—photos of the original marker, scans of the Monarch Society records, and manipulated blueprints. Meanwhile, Amelia wrote a formal complaint to the council, citing zoning laws and the absence of her signature. They reviewed the letter three times before sealing it in an envelope. It would be delivered first thing tomorrow.

The wheels of justice had been slow, but they were moving now.

The inn grew quiet as dusk deepened. Amelia lit a lantern and stepped onto the porch, gazing toward the treeline. The fence stood still in the dimming light, a false witness to years of deceit. But now, thanks to Lady Grey's instincts and Clara's determination, it would soon tell a different story.

Lady Grey curled beside her chair, eyes half-lidded but alert. Her soft purring was like a drumbeat of promise—a promise that truth, though often buried, would always find its way back to the surface.

Chapter 27

Paper Trail

Midday light spilled through the bookshop's bay windows, catching in the dust motes and illuminating shelves crammed with everything from antique atlases to water-damaged romance novels. Clara Henderson sat behind the counter, ostensibly finishing the inventory on a shipment of gardening almanacs, but her eyes kept drifting to the manila folder tucked beneath the register. It was the folder she had retrieved just hours earlier from the backroom printer—documents that, if verified, could upend everything she and Amelia had worked to protect.

Her fingers drummed on the edge of the counter. Her tea had gone cold. Every few moments she glanced at the door, half-expecting someone to barge in and demand the evidence. The sense of being watched wasn't new—but now it came paired with a growing certainty: the danger wasn't just theoretical. It was real. It was here.

She'd found the emails almost by accident. A glitchy search had led her to an old admin account on the bookshop's network, one she occasionally used to print receipts for custom orders. Buried among archived correspondence between the Historical Preservation Committee and the Garden Festival organizers was a chain of emails from the past three months—between Vincent Pike and someone cryptically signed "M. Harrow."

Clara pulled out the folder and flipped it open again. The emails were cloaked in polished, vague business language—"strategic acquisition," "expedited approval," "long-term development viability"—but the implications were undeniable. Vincent had been coordinating behind the scenes, not just with local officials, but with a development firm aiming to acquire the Tumblebrook Inn and the surrounding land.

The final email chilled her. Dated just two weeks ago, it read:

Once the last parcel is acquired, our firm can proceed with Phase II. Ensure the property owner remains unaware until the final zoning revision is approved. All previous adjustments have gone unnoticed—keep it that way.

Clara's brow furrowed. She'd known Vincent was sleazy. But this? This was coordinated fraud.

She was still absorbing the scope of it when the bell above the bookshop door jingled.

Startled, she shoved the folder under the counter. It was only Mrs. Mellinger from the bakery, waving a copy of *Tumblebrook's Edible Flowers* and asking about a new delivery. Clara mustered a polite smile, rang up her purchase, and sent her off with a warm goodbye. As soon as the door closed, she locked the front latch and drew the blinds.

She pulled out her phone and dialed Amelia.

"Clara?" Amelia's voice came through breathless. "Is everything okay?"

"I found something," Clara said. "Emails between Vincent and a developer. The inn is just part of it. They've redrawn zoning maps without telling you."

A pause. "Meet me in the sunroom. Now."

* * *

The sunroom at Tumblebrook Inn was warm and quiet, its tall windows facing the back gardens and the treeline beyond. Amelia paced as Clara spread the printouts across the coffee table. Lady Grey perched on the windowsill, tail flicking as she watched a squirrel dart across the lawn.

Amelia scanned the emails, lips pressed tight.

"They're laying the groundwork for a commercial annex," Clara said. "Shops, maybe a parking lot. They're counting on the inn's land to unify the project."

"Without my knowledge?" Amelia snapped. "That's fraud. It's illegal."

Clara pointed to a line in the thread. "They think they can get away with it because they forged your compliance on the rezoning documents. The signature doesn't match yours, but unless someone looks closely—"

"We'll make them look closely. We've got more than enough to bring this to the council."

"I was thinking bigger," Clara said. "Leak it to the paper. Make it public before the final vote. They won't risk going through with it if everyone's watching."

Amelia hesitated. "That could paint a target on the inn. On us."

"We're already on their radar. At this point, it's safer to shine a light on everything."

Lady Grey meowed and leapt gracefully to the floor, circling once before hopping onto the table and placing her paw on a document.

Amelia smiled faintly. "She has excellent instincts."

"She really does," Clara agreed. Then, more seriously: "There's one more name. M. Harrow. No title, no affiliation. But they seem to be pulling strings."

"Could be a fake name. Or someone from the Monarch Society."

Clara tapped her chin. "It's possible. And if it is, we're up against more than just Pike's ambition. We're up against legacy."

The room fell silent.

"Then we go to Mr. Lark," Amelia said. "If anyone knows who Harrow is—or was—he will."

* * *

Gossamer Fables smelled of dust, old leather, and a faint trace of vanilla from an ancient diffuser tucked behind the counter. Mr. Lark greeted them with a raised eyebrow and a knowing smile, as though he'd been expecting them.

"Ladies," he said. "Is this about the papers I noticed missing from our archive log?"

Clara and Amelia exchanged a glance.

"We found one of them," Clara admitted. "And a whole lot more. We need help identifying someone."

She passed him a printout from the email thread. Mr. Lark adjusted his glasses.

"M. Harrow... That's a name I haven't seen in years. Marcus Harrow. Part of the second wave of Monarch Society investors. Died a long time ago."

Amelia frowned. "Then this can't be him."

"A descendant, perhaps. Or someone borrowing the name. In Tumblebrook, both are plausible."

Clara leaned in. "What did Marcus Harrow want?"

"Control," Lark said. "He believed the town's history gave him the right to shape its future. He pushed for heritage-based zoning policies —ones that prioritized early-development families."

"Like Vincent's," Clara murmured.

Lark nodded.

"Do you have any of Harrow's writings? Letters? Journals? Anything that might prove a connection?"

Mr. Lark disappeared into the back. When he returned, he carried a slim folio and a thick leather-bound notebook.

"These haven't been touched in decades. But I think they're exactly what you need."

* * *

That night, back at the inn, Clara pored over the notebook beneath the soft glow of a reading lamp. Lady Grey curled beside her, purring softly. The sound of Amelia typing filled the room.

The entries were meticulous. Plans. Maps. Land records. And commentary laced with unsettling ideology—preserving lineage, guarding historical rights, fencing out outsiders.

One passage stood out:

The ridge line must remain Monarch-controlled. If any section falls outside the legacy circle, the continuity collapses. Move boundary lines as needed. History is pliable to those who write it.

Clara looked up. "It's not just about money. It never was. It's about control. Rewriting the town's foundation."

Amelia turned from her desk. "Then it's time we write a new chapter. With the truth in every line."

The room fell quiet, save for Lady Grey's rhythmic purring. They both knew they weren't just facing down a development scheme. They were confronting a legacy of deception.

And they were about to bring the whole thing into the light.

<h1 style="text-align:center">Chapter 28</h1>

<h2 style="text-align:center">Secrets in the Shed</h2>

The rain had stopped, but the air still held the hush of something unfinished. Amelia Farnsworth walked briskly across the back garden, flashlight in hand and her wool shawl pulled tight around her shoulders. The scent of damp earth mingled with lingering spring hyacinths, and in the distance, the lake whispered quietly against its banks. The Tumblebrook Inn loomed behind her, its warm windows flickering with candlelight and muffled conversation—a sharp contrast to the darkened trail she followed toward Vincent Pike's rented cottage.

She paused at the treeline, breath visible in the chilled air. It was nearing midnight, and the weight of secrets hung low across the yard like morning fog. Clara was inside, keeping watch at the front entrance in case Vincent returned early from his supposed meeting in Duluth. Lady Grey, unusually restless, had pawed twice at the shed door earlier that evening, her amber eyes locked on the handle.

That had been enough to convince Amelia to act.

She crept along the side path, boots squishing in the soft earth. The shed stood at the rear of the cottage, its paint flaking and latch rusted. It didn't match the modern trim of the house and looked as though it had stood there long before Vincent arrived. She cast one last glance toward the house. No lights. No sounds. No movement behind the curtains. She pressed on, heart thrumming.

The latch clicked open with a reluctant creak. She eased the door forward, revealing stale air and the faint scent of fertilizer, oil, and damp cedar. Amelia slipped inside, closing the door quietly behind her. Her flashlight beam swept the narrow room: shelves stacked with labeled bins, a row of gardening tools, a broken bench—and in the corner, something that made her chest tighten.

A patch of gray fur.

She knelt and picked up the soft tuft, rolling it gently between her fingers. It was unmistakably Lady Grey's. And beside it, half-buried under a dusty trowel, lay the broken bell from her collar.

Her heart clenched. "You were here," she whispered, voice catching.

Lady Grey had clawed her way free—but not before being held here. Judging by the faint indentations in the dust, she'd tried to signal. Amelia rose and examined the area, noting shallow claw marks and a spot where dust had been disturbed in a vague circular pattern. She lifted a loose board—and gasped.

Beneath it lay a rolled-up printout. She unfurled it: a detailed satellite map of the Tumblebrook Inn's property. Not just a survey—it was annotated. Bright red markings denoted fence lines, under-ground piping, and projected building zones.

At the bottom of the sheet, typed in blocky font: *Reclamation Phase—Pending Authorization.*

This was it. Proof Vincent and his collaborators had been planning to seize control—not just of the inn, but the land beneath it.

She tucked the map into her coat and continued searching. Behind a half-emptied seed bag lay a stack of real estate brochures—mockups of townhomes and boutique storefronts where the garden and orchard currently stood. Upscale. Sterile. Devoid of the soul Tumblebrook was built on.

Her breath caught—a twig snapped outside.

She doused her flashlight and crouched, ears straining. Another sound—a footstep. Then silence.

Someone was out there.

She waited, still as the tools on the wall, until the footsteps faded. Then, cautiously, she slipped from the shed and hurried back to the inn.

Clara was waiting in the parlor, a steaming mug of chamomile in hand. Amelia handed her the tuft of fur, the broken bell, and the map.

Clara's eyes widened. "You were right. He had her. And this... this is his plan."

"Not anymore," Amelia said, her voice steady.

Lady Grey sauntered into the room, brushing against Amelia's legs before hopping into Clara's lap.

Amelia smiled. "You started all this. Now let's finish it."

The next morning dawned cloudy, mist clinging to the windows like a veil. In the office behind the inn's front desk, Amelia and Clara laid out their evidence. The map, brochures, fur, and bell—a narrative was forming.

"Let's overlay this with the property survey we did near the orchard," Clara said, pulling a folder from beneath guest receipts. "See this line?"

Amelia nodded. "That's where we found the fence discrepancy."

"And here," Clara said, tapping the annotated map from the shed, "is the proposed road for the new townhomes. Right through the orchard and across your herb garden."

Amelia sat back, stunned. "They've already planned it down to the concrete."

"And this brochure," Clara added, flipping one open, "says completion by next spring. That's aggressive, even for developers."

"They must think they've already won."

Clara gave a tight-lipped smile. "They didn't factor in Lady Grey."

They shared a laugh, but the weight of conspiracy still loomed.

"I'm going back," Amelia said suddenly. "To the shed. I didn't check the loft."

"Amelia, we have enough," Clara said cautiously.

"Not yet. There might be more—something that ties Vincent to the Monarch Society directly."

Clara hesitated, then nodded. "Take the walkie. I'll stay tuned."

Amelia returned to the shed under the guise of delivering preserves. Vincent was still away—a sticky note on the door confirmed it.

Inside the shed again, she climbed onto the broken bench and peered into the small loft above. Dark, dusty, and scented faintly of cedar. She reached up and pulled down a small wooden crate.

Inside: a leather-bound ledger, several rolled scrolls, and a worn Monarch Society pin—the same butterfly she and Clara had seen in the blueprints.

The ledger was filled with crisp, deliberate handwriting. Dates. Signatures. References to land parcels throughout Tumblebrook. Most damning were the names: Vincent Pike, M. Harrow, and several town officials.

Amelia photographed every page. She slipped the pin into her pocket.

Back at the inn, Clara scanned the images. "This... this ledger is the smoking gun. It's the Monarch Society's playbook."

"They've infiltrated every part of our town," Amelia said softly. "It's more than greed. It's control."

Lady Grey leapt onto the desk, pawing at one of the photos.

Clara chuckled. "Looks like she approves."

Amelia looked at her friend. "We bring this to Mr. Lark. He'll know what to do."

Clara nodded. "Let's take down the Monarch Society, again."

Chapter 29

A Codex of Clues

The early morning sunlight filtered softly through the stained-glass transom windows of Gossamer Fables, painting flickers of color across the mahogany floorboards. Clara Henderson stood behind the counter, sorting through a crate of returned books with mechanical precision. Her mind, however, was miles away—still tangled in the whirlwind of documents, deeds, and secrets that had upended her once-quiet world. The ledger from Vincent's shed had cracked the case wide open, yet questions still bloomed like stubborn weeds, clinging to the edges of her thoughts.

A flutter of petals on the display table caught her eye.

She paused. The centerpiece of the bookshop's festival display—a vibrant bouquet of irises, daffodils, marigolds, and an unusual variety of blue hyacinths—stood proudly in the center of the room. Delivered by Melvin the gardener two days prior, it was part of his contribution to the Tumblebrook Garden Festival's "Floral Through the Ages" showcase.

Clara's brow furrowed.

She circled the arrangement slowly. Something about the layering of the colors, the order of the stems, and the symmetrical repetition along the rim of the vase struck her as too precise. It looked familiar. Deliberate. Monarch deliberate.

She pulled out her notebook and quickly sketched the floral pattern. Cross-referencing it with the cipher patterns in the Monarch Society ledger, she gasped. The floral positioning—when viewed from above—mimicked the butterfly insignia. Not just in shape, but numerically: each flower type appeared in grouped repetitions of three, seven, or eleven. Prime numbers. The same sequence used in the Monarch map legends.

"Oh, Melvin," she whispered. "What have you stumbled into?"

She left the shop in a hurry, sketchpad under her arm. The town square buzzed with the day's energy—music, laughter, the scent of scones wafting from Doris's café—but Clara moved through it like a woman with blinders. Her destination was clear.

She found Melvin trimming a bonsai under a striped canopy.

"Clara! You're just in time to watch me prepare to prune. I've got shears sharp enough to—"

"Melvin," she interrupted gently. "I need to ask you about the flower arrangements—especially the one for Gossamer Fables."

He blinked. "That one? Just something I threw together. Found a diagram in an old gardening manual someone donated to the community shed. Thought it looked nice."

Clara's pulse quickened. "Do you still have the diagram?"

"Should be in my notebook somewhere. Want to have a look?"

He handed her a dog-eared spiral notebook filled with dirt-smudged sketches and clippings. Tucked inside was a parchment floral diagram annotated in tight cursive script. At the bottom, faintly inked, was the Monarch Society's butterfly crest.

Clara's stomach turned.

"This diagram isn't decorative," she said. "It's a cipher."

Melvin scratched his head. "A what now?"

Clara sat on a nearby bench, pulling out the ledger photos and her notebook. She began cross-referencing the flower placement and notations, translating their arrangement. The hyacinths mirrored numerical values tied to land plots. The daffodils marked a border. The whole design spelled out coordinates.

Coordinates pointing directly to the ridge behind the Tumblebrook Inn.

Her hand trembled slightly.

Lady Grey had clawed a warning beneath the floor. The ridge had been the site of the fence tampering. Now this cipher pointed there too. Everything connected.

"Melvin," Clara said, voice low, "where exactly did you find this diagram?"

"In a binder someone left in the town archives. Most of it was junk. That page just stood out."

"Do you still have the binder?"

"Could be in the archive room behind the council chambers."

"I need to see it."

Later that afternoon, Clara slipped behind the council chambers using her spare key—the one Amelia insisted all bookshop managers should have. The archive room smelled of old ink and lemon polish. Dust floated in slanted beams of light as Clara scanned shelf after shelf.

And there it was: a thick green binder with the Monarch butterfly embossed in faded gold on the spine.

Inside were more floral diagrams, cipher wheels, land plats, and festival documents. The Monarch Society had embedded their codes in plain sight—through rituals, horticulture, even pageantry. Every Garden Festival had been part of the puzzle.

She found a photograph—sepia-toned, curling at the edges—of a younger Melvin flanked by what appeared to be a reenactment group. Several wore lapel pins with the butterfly crest. The gardeners of Tumblebrook had unknowingly continued Monarch traditions.

Clara photographed every page and carefully returned the binder.

Back at the inn, she spread her findings on the kitchen table. Amelia and Lady Grey listened as she spoke.

"We focused on deeds and ledgers. But the Society left clues in everything. Even flowers."

Amelia leaned in. "So this year's festival became a message?"

"Not intentionally. But the tools were there. Melvin just followed instructions without knowing their origin."

Lady Grey leapt onto the table and pawed at the floral map sketch, circling the ridge.

"She agrees," Amelia said with a faint smile.

Clara met her gaze. "We need to go. Tonight."

Amelia nodded. "I'll get the lanterns."

Clara looked down at her notebook, heart pounding. The Society's web had grown wider—but they were close. As close as they'd ever been.

Their boots crunched over fallen leaves as night fell. Lanterns swung in their hands. Stars blinked overhead. Clara didn't look up.

Her eyes were fixed forward—on the path, on the ridge, on the truth that lay just ahead.

Chapter 30

The Journal in the Wall

The morning sun crept through the curtains of Amelia Farnsworth's bedroom, casting delicate gold threads across the floral quilt. But sleep had long since abandoned her. Her mind churned with images from the night before—the strange symbols etched into stones atop the ridge, the symmetrical placement of moss-covered boulders, and the silent understanding she and Clara had shared beneath the stars. Every breath of air on that ridge had felt charged, like the land itself was holding its breath, waiting to be acknowledged. The breeze had carried whispers that didn't quite belong to the night. And most chilling of all was the quiet revelation etched near the base of the largest boulder: a symbol matching the Monarch butterfly.

She rubbed her tired eyes and was about to swing her legs out of bed when a soft tapping reached her ears—distinct, rhythmic. Lady Grey, her ever-intuitive companion, pawed with unusual insistence at the baseboard of the east-facing wall. Her sleek grey tail swished with purpose.

Amelia sat up straighter. "What is it now, darling?" she

murmured, slipping her feet into worn slippers and padding over. Lady Grey let out a low, urgent chirp and resumed her scratching.

Kneeling beside her, Amelia brushed her fingers along the painted surface. Her touch paused on a faint seam running the length of the baseboard—subtle, but different. The texture felt wrong. The inn was old, and she'd always chalked up its quirks to history, but this... this was deliberate.

She stood quickly, fetched a screwdriver from the kitchen drawer, and returned, heart thumping. With gentle pressure, she pried at the paneling. A soft creak echoed in the stillness, and the section gave way, revealing a narrow hollow in the wall. A cloud of dust drifted into the air, and inside, wrapped in oilcloth and bound with brittle twine, was a small leather-bound book.

"Clara," Amelia called, breathless. "You need to see this."

Within minutes, Clara arrived, hair tousled from sleep and notepad in hand. Her expression shifted from curiosity to awe.

"It's her handwriting," Amelia whispered, untying the twine reverently. "Annie Farnsworth."

The first page bore a neat inscription in delicate script: To be opened only when the land begins to whisper once more.

They exchanged a glance. Lady Grey leapt onto the armrest, her amber eyes fixed on the journal.

The entries dated back decades—some postwar, others during the inn's leanest seasons. Amelia read aloud while Clara jotted notes, gasping as the story of the land's guardianship unfolded in ink.

One entry read: "Tonight, we met beneath the orchard pines. Seven of us—keepers of the ridge, watchers of the lines. We've known the Monarch patterns longer than they think. We marked the stones ourselves. We hid them beneath festival blooms and council petitions. If ever they return—those who seek to carve profit from heritage—this journal must guide them back to truth."

Another: "They came with papers, stamped and false. Offered me a sum I could never match, but I would not yield. I walked the perimeter at dawn, and the fence had moved. Clara's great-grandfather confirmed it—stolen inches at a time."

Clara looked up sharply. "My family was involved in this?"

"It seems so," Amelia said softly. "Your great-grandfather stood with Annie to protect the ridge."

The journal named names—Melvin, Doris, even Mr. Lark's grandfather. The town had been protected by quiet stewards for generations, many of whom had no idea of their shared legacy.

"Listen," Amelia said, eyes scanning a later entry. "If the lines ever vanish completely, go to the shelf behind the guest registry. There's a hidden compartment with the old blueprints. They show the inn before the shifting started."

They rushed downstairs and shoved the heavy registry shelf aside. Clara's fingers found a groove in the paneling. With a click, a false back opened to reveal a roll of yellowed blueprints.

They unrolled them on the kitchen table. The plans detailed the inn and surrounding grounds—including the orchard, ridge, and winding lakeside trail—but most importantly, the original fence line. It had undeniably been moved.

"Look here," Clara said, pointing. "The ridge marks weren't decorative. They were land markers. This proves someone's been trying to alter the boundaries."

"And this," Amelia said, tracing a trail from the ridge to the lake. "It matches the path where we saw the shadowy figure that night."

Lady Grey, ever the sentinel, circled the blueprint and stopped at a butterfly symbol etched near the tool shed.

"She's showing us something," Amelia said. "That symbol's Monarch."

The late morning sun streamed in, casting a warm glow over the plans, the journal, and the faces of the two women hunched over them.

"We were meant to find this," Clara murmured.

"All of it connects—the stones, the ciphered flowers, the journal, the fence line... even the missing deed pages," Amelia added. "This land is worth more than money. It's rooted in memory, in guardianship."

They spent the afternoon documenting everything: the journal entries, blueprint measurements, and transcriptions of the codes Lady Grey had previously clawed beneath the crawlspace. They included the moss alignment on the ridge, which now seemed less like natural growth and more like intentional placement. By dusk, the evidence spanned nearly the entire dining table, pinned down by teacups, paperweights, and salt shakers.

Later that evening, as crickets began to chirp and fireflies blinked into being, Amelia sat on the porch with Lady Grey curled beside her. She opened the journal again, running her fingers over the fading ink.

"Thank you, Aunt Annie," she whispered.

The breeze rustled the hedges. The inn's wind chimes sang a gentle song.

Clara joined her, two mugs of chamomile tea in hand. "You think we're ready?"

"We have to be," Amelia replied. "They've taken too much already."

"We should go public. Soon."

"We will," Amelia said. "But first, let's follow Annie's map. One more time. We owe her that much."

Lady Grey stretched languidly, flicking her tail as if in agreement.

The following day, the Tumblebrook Town Hall buzzed with curiosity. Word had spread—Amelia and Clara had requested the floor during the open forum segment of the council meeting, claiming they had evidence of wrongdoing that the town needed to see.

The chamber filled with townspeople. Mr. Lark sat near the back with Melvin. Doris arrived with a tray of lemon bars, distributing them to the crowd like it was any other bake sale.

Mayor Keegan adjusted his glasses and tapped the gavel. "Miss Farnsworth, you have the floor."

Amelia stepped forward, blueprints in hand. Clara followed with the journal and a stack of photocopied pages.

"We've come not just with accusations," Amelia began, "but with proof. Proof that the land surrounding the Tumblebrook Inn has been fraudulently marked for commercial development by parties misrepresenting both town records and history."

A murmur swept through the room.

Clara stepped beside her. "We found altered blueprints. Secret ledgers. A decades-old journal from Annie Farnsworth confirming a long legacy of tampering and manipulation by what we now know to be remnants of the Monarch Society."

Gasps met the name. People glanced at one another.

Amelia laid out the blueprints, pointing to mismatched fence lines. "These changes were gradual, hidden beneath the guise of maintenance or beautification. But every inch stolen chipped away at our history."

Clara opened the journal. "Annie's entries describe meetings with town founders, secret codes hidden in festival layouts, and plans to protect the land from those who would rewrite its purpose."

Mayor Keegan leaned forward. "And who, exactly, do you accuse?"

Amelia inhaled. "Vincent Pike. M. Harrow—descendant or impersonator. And those complicit in allowing altered zoning to pass without scrutiny."

Mr. Lark stood. "I corroborate their findings. I've seen the documents myself."

More murmurs. Faces turned toward council members.

Amelia held up a photo of the Monarch butterfly seal found beneath the inn. "The Society never disappeared. It just changed names, found new ways to blend in. But we've brought their intentions into the light."

Lady Grey, sitting quietly at Clara's feet, let out a firm meow. The crowd laughed—but it broke the tension.

Mayor Keegan looked thoughtful. "The council will review these materials thoroughly. But rest assured—if these claims hold up, the vote on zoning will be suspended. And charges may follow."

A surge of hope pulsed through the room.

Outside, as townsfolk lingered in clusters, Amelia and Clara stood beneath the maple tree near the front steps.

"We did it," Clara said, stunned.

Amelia nodded. "And we're not done yet. There's more to uncover. But at least now, the town is awake."

Lady Grey purred loudly, as if to say: Finally.

Chapter 31

The Symbol Beneath the Root

Lady Grey slunk through the damp hush of early morning, the dew dampening her sleek gray coat as she trotted along the back gardens of the Tumblebrook Inn. Her amber eyes, always alert, flicked toward the line of pine trees that bordered the property. She had ventured out before anyone else had stirred, following the persistent whisper of instinct. Something called to her —something buried. Something waiting.

The ground still smelled of yesterday's rain, rich and earthy. The cat's paws were soundless on the soft mulch as she crept through the hedgerow and crossed into the outer yard. Here, where the land began to tangle itself into thicket and slope, lay an old tree stump split from a lightning strike decades ago. A forgotten landmark, gnarled and dark, remembered by none but her.

She paused. Her nose twitched.

A scent lingered—faint but distinct. Not human. Not quite animal either. A mixture of cedar, paper, and iron. Familiar in a way only Lady Grey could decipher. She padded toward the stump and hopped onto its cracked surface, tail swishing. Her claws flexed into the decayed wood, tugging loose strips. Something creaked beneath.

She jumped down and began to dig with determined precision. Her front paws swept mulch and dirt aside in practiced rhythm. The earth gave way to something hard. Her claws scraped metal. She paused, ears erect.

A box.

She pressed her weight against it, loosening the soil around its edges until the top groaned under the pressure. A rusted latch jutted from the front like a crooked tooth. She batted at it. It clinked.

It took her some effort, but her paws, nimble and deliberate, worked until she'd unearthed most of the container. Mud splattered across her face, but she didn't flinch. She paused to peer upward, sensing the wind shift, her amber eyes narrowing at the rustling trees. She could feel time stirring with the scent—something old was awakening.

Lady Grey gave a low, purposeful meow and turned back the way she came, leaving a trail of pawprints pressed into the damp earth. The morning sun began to lift the shadows from the garden.

Back at the inn, Clara and Amelia were finishing their tea when Lady Grey appeared at the kitchen door, her fur streaked with dirt and moss. She gave a sharp meow and turned tail without waiting.

"She's up to something," Clara said, rising from her chair.

"She's always up to something," Amelia replied, setting down her cup. But she was already grabbing her cardigan.

Lady Grey led them with the air of a general, glancing over her shoulder every few feet. They followed her beyond the garden path, through the briars, and to the battered stump.

Amelia crouched first. "What on earth..."

The soil was freshly disturbed. Clara retrieved a trowel from the shed and began to dig. Soon, they unearthed the box—rusted, weathered, but unmistakably sealed.

Clara brushed off the top and studied the corroded engraving. "Look. That symbol. It's the same butterfly from the Monarch Society blueprints."

With effort, they opened the lid. Inside were scrolls of parchment, brittle with age, along with several worn leather-bound ledgers and an envelope stamped with the seal of the original Tumblebrook land council.

"These are...land deeds," Amelia whispered, delicately lifting a sheaf from the box. "Old ones. From before the last revision."

Clara's brow furrowed as she read the names. "These parcels— some of them border the inn. This one lists the Farnsworth name."

"That's Aunt Annie's signature."

They exchanged a glance, the weight of realization settling between them in a heavy silence.

Amelia gently unfolded another document, dated nearly seventy years ago. The ink was faded, but clear enough. A hand-drawn boundary line looped around the inn, including land currently marked as belonging to the Pike estate.

"She knew," Amelia murmured. "She knew it was being taken from us. That's why she hid the journal, the maps, everything."

Clara nodded. "And she wasn't alone. Look—these notes reference meetings. Secret gatherings held to resist land re-zoning. This wasn't just a personal grudge. This was a movement."

Amelia thumbed through one of the ledgers. Inside were columns of dates, names, and cryptic codes next to meeting entries. At the bottom, scrawled in shaky cursive, was a phrase: *The truth roots deeper than any fence line.*

Lady Grey hopped onto the stump once again, tail flicking. Clara scratched behind her ears. "You brilliant cat. You've found what the rest of us have been stumbling toward."

They carried the box back to the inn. In the quiet of the library room, they spread the documents across a long table and began cataloging the contents.

Among the papers were aerial photographs, annotations from historical surveys, and personal letters between landowners. The tone grew more urgent with each decade—warnings about fraudulent rezoning, pressure from unnamed developers, and veiled threats.

One letter, dated only fifteen years ago, bore the same hand-writing as Aunt Annie's journal:

"The Monarch have returned, hiding behind new names and friendly smiles. But their goals haven't changed. I fear what will happen if we let them win this time. The inn must remain untouched —it is the key."

"This proves everything," Clara whispered. "Vincent Pike isn't just opportunistic—he's continuing an old scheme. A long-standing effort to seize this land for profit."

Amelia's expression was steel. "Then we'll stop him. And we'll use every document, every name, every root we've uncovered. We owe it to Annie—and to everyone who tried before us."

Lady Grey let out a soft trill, curling up between the maps like a guardian.

* * *

Later that evening, they invited Ezra the Hermit and Mr. Lark to review the materials. Both men gasped at the scope of what had been uncovered.

"The Monarch Society," Mr. Lark said, adjusting his glasses. "They were thought to be dissolved. But clearly—"

"They just changed their wings," Ezra finished grimly.

They laid out a plan: to present the findings to the town council, to rally allies, and—if needed—to involve the press. But first, they needed to secure the documents.

In a newly cleaned cupboard beneath the inn's staircase, Amelia placed the rusted box behind a false panel—just as Aunt Annie had done with her journal years before.

But the night did not end in silence. As Amelia locked the cupboard, Clara held up one more page they hadn't yet examined—a list of names, handwritten in two columns. One labeled TRUSTED. The other, DANGEROUS.

Several names they knew were there. Some they did not.

And at the bottom of the dangerous list: Vincent Pike.

As night fell, Amelia stood once more by the kitchen window. The garden shimmered in moonlight, serene.

And yet, beneath the calm, she now knew—just as Lady Grey had sensed all along—there was a quiet war for the soul of the land.

A war they had just begun to win.

Chapter 32

Documents Don't Lie

The late afternoon sun filtered through the high windows of the Tumblebrook Inn's library, casting golden rectangles over the weathered pages scattered across the long oak table. Clara leaned over a stack of historical documents, her brows drawn tight with focus. The air smelled of ink, dust, aged parchment, and resolve. Her hands, ink-smudged and meticulous, worked steadily through the pile of old ledgers, land grants, and annotated survey maps that covered nearly every inch of the table.

"I still can't believe this box existed just a few feet from our garden," she murmured, her voice barely above a whisper. Lady Grey, curled on the arm of the nearby settee, replied with a soft purr, her tail flicking lazily in rhythm with the ticking of the mantle clock.

Clara had cataloged over thirty individual documents that morning, but the one currently spread before her was the most critical: a property deed dated March 3, 1956—bearing the official seal of the Tumblebrook Land Registry Office. The name at the top read: Annette Farnsworth. The document clearly defined property boundaries that included the land where Vincent Pike's garden and pavilion now stood.

She sat back slowly, letting the weight of the discovery settle into her bones. "This predates every one of Pike's claims," she said softly, her voice tinged with disbelief and rising resolve.

Just then, Amelia entered, balancing a tray with two steaming mugs of tea and a plate of shortbread cookies dusted with powdered sugar. "Progress?"

Clara accepted a mug and blew gently on the surface before sipping. "That's one way to put it. Amelia, this deed alone upends everything Pike's asserted about his property lines. It's not just speculation anymore. It's fact."

Amelia set the tray down and leaned over Clara's shoulder, her gaze narrowing. "That's her handwriting," she said, pointing to the elegant script at the bottom. "She dotted her i's with little butterflies. Aunt Annie always said even legal work needed flair."

Clara smiled faintly, then pointed to a survey map she'd pinned open beside the deed. "Here's the clincher. This map came with the same set of documents. It's clearly marked with the original boundary posts—long before any rezoning occurred. See this line?" She traced a finger along the faded ink. "It pushes the boundary almost fifteen feet further west than what's reflected in today's maps."

Amelia's eyes widened. "That would mean—"

"Vincent Pike has built part of his landscaping and the garden pavilion over property that legally belongs to you. The inn's land. He's been encroaching without legal right."

They sat in silence, the air heavy with implications. This wasn't just about town rivalries or a missing pet. This was deliberate, systematic theft.

"I want to bring in someone official," Clara said. "Someone neutral. Maybe from the historical society or a licensed surveyor who hasn't been involved in town politics."

Amelia nodded. "Agreed. We need confirmation. And we'll need to be careful. If Pike suspects what we've found, he'll try to get ahead of it. Or erase it."

Lady Grey stretched and leapt down from the settee. She trotted to the doorway and paused, tail flicking with purpose.

"She wants us to follow her again," Amelia said, already rising.

Clara raised an eyebrow. "Should we be concerned that a cat has taken over our investigative strategy?"

"Possibly."

They followed Lady Grey through the garden and up the hill toward the bookshop. Mr. Lark was closing up for the evening but paused when he saw them approaching with a thick folder clutched in Clara's hands.

"Clara, Amelia," he greeted. "You both look like you're about to drop some very old secrets."

Inside, the shop smelled of old parchment, lemon oil, and a hint of cinnamon. Clara laid the deed on the counter with the reverence of sacred text. Mr. Lark examined it carefully, then moved to his filing drawer.

"I thought I remembered something... Yes, here we are." He produced a brittle, yellowed page. "This is the duplicate of that same deed, kept here since 1956. Look—they match exactly."

Amelia leaned in. "This proves she filed it properly. And the registry should have a record of this."

"They should," Mr. Lark agreed. "But many older documents were never transferred when records went digital. Some vanished altogether."

Clara's jaw tightened. "That makes it easier for people like Pike to manipulate timelines. If no one checks the paper trail, they're left to rewrite history digitally."

"Would you mind if I made copies?" Mr. Lark asked.

"Please do. And keep one in your shop's attic archive—the really hidden one," Clara said.

Back at the inn that night, Clara scanned every page into a secure USB drive and uploaded encrypted versions to a password-protected cloud account. "I don't trust local systems anymore," she said. "If Pike's willing to erase land history, he's capable of erasing files."

The next morning, Clara placed a call to Lauren Penmark, a respected independent surveyor. "I'll be there by tomorrow afternoon," Lauren said. "Send me what you've got."

Just then, the doorbell chimed. Amelia opened it to find a courier holding a manila envelope. No return address. No logo.

"For Clara Henderson," the courier said before briskly departing.

Clara slit it open. Inside was a single sheet. Typed. Unmarked. Threatening.

Don't get too comfortable with truths that were meant to stay buried. You won't like what else comes to light.

Her hand trembled.

Amelia stepped beside her. "What is it?"

Clara handed over the note. Her throat was tight.

Lady Grey let out a sharp, disapproving meow.

"Well," Clara said, her voice hardening, "I guess we're getting close."

And for the first time, the quiet halls of the Tumblebrook Inn felt like a vault of resistance. Documents didn't lie—people did. But not this time.

Chapter 33

Town Council Games

The Tumblebrook Town Hall had witnessed many spirited debates over the years—classic small-town spats about parade routes, jam-judging criteria, and fiercely contested floral arrangements. Yet on this particular Thursday evening, a heavier tension simmered beneath the surface. Gone were the light-hearted squabbles of festivals past. In their place lingered a quiet, growing unrest—a low thrum of suspicion that whispered through the crowd like wind before a storm.

Amelia Farnsworth stood just outside the hall, her hand resting lightly on the worn brass handle of the double doors. She inhaled deeply, straightened her blazer, and pushed forward. The heavy door creaked as it opened, revealing a hall filled with a buzzing crowd that fell into a hush as she entered.

Her footsteps echoed across the polished floorboards as she moved toward the back. Familiar faces turned to look—some curious, some wary. Murmurs trailed in her wake. The scent of strong coffee and lemon bars from the refreshment table mingled with the nerves floating through the air.

Tonight's town council meeting had been added to the schedule only days earlier, and its vague agenda was all the invitation Tumble-brook needed for full attendance. Rumors had spread like wildfire: land disputes, forged papers, mysterious behavior. And for once, the whispers weren't just about missing pastries at Doris Finch's café.

Every seat had been claimed. Locals old and new lined the walls, some standing on tiptoe for a better view, others holding clipboards or phones poised for notes or photos. Folding chairs borrowed from the senior center had been brought in to supplement the pew-style seating.

Lady Grey, sensing the mood earlier that day, had chosen to remain at the inn curled up in the sunniest window ledge she could find—far from political tension, but not forgotten.

Clara sat near the front, her expression unreadable. Her cardigan —a calming shade of blue—was paired with a tidy white blouse, and a slim folder rested across her knees like a shield. She didn't wave when Amelia approached, but her eyes flicked briefly in recognition.

"Feels more like the opening act of a courtroom drama than a town council meeting," Amelia whispered as she took the seat beside her.

Clara's lips twitched, though she didn't smile. "Let's just hope we don't end up as Exhibit A."

Vincent Pike lounged three rows ahead, legs crossed, looking entirely too relaxed. His sharp suit and gleaming lapel pin made him stand out amidst the sea of flannel and cardigans. He chatted amiably with Nancy Corwin, who appeared less confident—her notebook clutched tightly in both hands.

At exactly seven, Mayor Keegan rose, adjusted his tie, and approached the podium. The microphone offered a piercing squeal before settling.

"Good evening, everyone," he began, his voice practiced but strained. "Thank you for joining us. We have several topics to address tonight, including the final reports from the Garden Festival, updates on Maple Creek fencing, and the item most of you are likely here for —land boundary appeals."

That last item caused a ripple of murmurs across the room. Council members stiffened. Eyes turned toward Vincent Pike.

The meeting opened as usual, with notes of appreciation and recaps. The Garden Festival had turned a modest profit. Donations exceeded expectations. Doris's lemon-thyme jam had, once again, claimed a blue ribbon. But underneath the pleasant formalities, anticipation brewed.

Finally, the mayor cleared his throat. "We now open the floor to comments on property surveys and zoning changes."

The room fell silent. Then, from somewhere near the back, a voice cut through the hush:

"What about the forged transfers and the fake stamps?" It was clear, unshaken—and entirely anonymous.

Gasps erupted. Several people turned in their seats. A teacup clattered to the floor.

Mayor Keegan blinked. "I—I'm sorry?"

"Vincent Pike's name appears more than once. On questionable permits. On deeds that don't match town archives."

Vincent paled. His eyes darted to Nancy, who looked stricken.

Amelia stood, her voice calm but firm. "Mr. Mayor, if I may, Clara and I have documentation to support these claims."

The mayor gestured her forward, relieved for structure amid chaos.

Clara joined her, holding the folder tightly. As they reached the podium, the crowd parted like tall grass in the wind.

Amelia opened to the first page. "This deed from 1956, signed by Annette Farnsworth, confirms the original property lines of the Tumblebrook Inn. These records have been validated by the historical society and appear in multiple copies."

She turned the page. "This next document—a modern permit bearing an outdated approval stamp—was submitted during the recent boundary adjustments. It's missing the required digital registration number."

Clara added, "The permit's physical ink doesn't match town-issued documents. We've cross-referenced with archived approvals from the last ten years. This one stands out—for all the wrong reasons."

A wave of whispers surged.

Vincent stood abruptly. "This is a smear campaign. Boundaries shift all the time in developing towns! This isn't fraud—it's flexibility."

Clara arched a brow. "Flexibility doesn't require deception."

Nancy Corwin stood next, her voice thin. "I—I was told the papers were pre-approved. I didn't double-check them. That was my error."

The mayor rubbed his temples. "Recess. Fifteen minutes. Council members, my office."

As council members filed out, conversations erupted in the hall. Phones buzzed. Neighbors whispered.

Clara leaned toward Amelia. "Do you think that anonymous voice was Ezra?"

Amelia shook her head slowly. "No. I think someone else has had enough of being quiet."

From the corner of the room, an elderly woman in a shawl muttered, "About time."

This wasn't just a town meeting anymore. It was a reckoning—for those who had kept secrets. For those who thought no one would ever dig beneath the surface.

And Tumblebrook, so long shielded by its idyllic charm, had just taken its first collective breath toward the truth.

Fallout came swiftly.

By the next morning, flyers appeared at the café, post office, and bookstore: "Town Lands. Town Truths. Transparency Meeting—Saturday at Dusk." Clara didn't print them. Neither did Amelia. The community had picked up the torch.

Nancy Corwin resigned from the zoning board by noon, issuing a public apology taped to the council hall doors.

Doris Finch started offering a "Truth Blend" tea at the café, and anyone caught gossiping too loudly was told to "put it in writing and bring it to the forum."

At the inn, curious guests asked to see the documents. Some wanted to help. Others simply brought food and listened.

And Vincent Pike? He disappeared—for two days.

When he returned, his easy smile was gone. He walked Main Street in silence. The lapel pin had vanished.

But Clara knew the reckoning wasn't over.

Because when she opened the inn's mailbox that evening, there was another note.

Typed. Anonymous.

You've rattled the nest. Watch what flies out next.

She tucked it into her pocket without a word.

"Let them come," she said softly.

The war for Tumblebrook's roots wasn't over. But its people had started to remember how deep those roots ran.

Chapter 34

The Gardener's Confession

The following morning broke over Tumblebrook with a deceptive softness, the kind that veiled unrest beneath a sky of pale blue. Early sunlight filtered through the lace curtains of the inn's kitchen, dappling the checkered floor in golden slants. Clara sat at the breakfast nook, her hands wrapped around a mug of strong black tea, but her thoughts were still entangled in the echoes of the previous night's town hall meeting. Vincent Pike's sputtering outrage, Nancy's quivering apology, the weight of Amelia's measured voice presenting the deeds—it felt like watching the crooked roots of a long-standing lie finally being pulled into the open.

Now, though, there was silence. Tumblebrook had settled into an uneasy stillness, like a town collectively holding its breath. Even the usual hum of morning—the burr of Doris's café grinder, the slow shuffle of dog walkers—was strangely subdued. Suspicion lingered in the air, delicate as frost.

Amelia entered quietly, her face pale but composed. She poured herself a cup of coffee, added only a splash of cream, and said, "Melvin left a message on the inn's voicemail. Said he needs to talk."

Clara raised an eyebrow. "This morning?"

"Said it couldn't wait."

They exchanged a glance, both knowing Melvin Jennings, the festival's gentle-hearted gardener, wasn't prone to haste. He tended to life like he did his plants—slow, careful, deliberate. For him to demand urgency meant something had finally bloomed past the point of containment.

Twenty minutes later, they stood at the edge of Melvin's plot behind the community greenhouse. The building, more shed than structure, leaned slightly, as if overwhelmed by years of soil and secrets. Trellises tangled with flowering vines framed the area, and the air was rich with the scent of damp loam, rusted iron, and lavender gone to seed.

Melvin stood beside a rose trellis, his hands sunk into the soil. He didn't look up right away.

"You came," he said finally.

"You asked us to," Amelia replied, her voice gentle but firm.

He nodded, pulling his hands free and wiping them on the faded green apron he always wore during planting season. "I've been sitting on this too long. I should've said something days ago. Maybe even last year. But I thought... well, I thought maybe it wouldn't matter."

Clara crossed her arms, a slow chill creeping up her spine. "Is this about the pawprints?"

Melvin flinched, confirming it before he spoke. "Yes. And more than that. It's about who told me to keep quiet."

He turned, motioning them toward the potting shed. Its frame creaked as they stepped inside, the air heavier here—earthy and close. Tools hung in neat rows on pegboards, but cobwebs had crept into the corners, and the light filtering through the dirty window was thick with dust.

Melvin gestured to a pair of overturned crates. "Might as well sit. What I have to say won't take long, but it won't be easy."

He leaned against the bench, his gaze focused on the floor. "I found the prints the morning after Lady Grey disappeared. Just near the edge of the maze. They were fresh, panicked. I followed them to my shed. Door was ajar. Inside was a mess—tools knocked over, bags of soil ripped open like something had scrambled to hide."

Clara's voice was tight. "And then?"

"Then Vincent Pike showed up."

Silence fell. Even the birds outside seemed to pause.

"He said things were 'delicate.' That the town couldn't afford hysteria. That the cat—Lady Grey—would be returned soon, so long as everyone stayed calm. And quiet. Then he handed me an envelope. Cash. Told me it was compensation for lost sleep, and that saying nothing would be the kindest thing I could do."

Amelia stepped forward. "You didn't report it?"

Melvin's shoulders slumped. "I took it. But I didn't spend it. I buried it beneath the fern pot behind the shed. Didn't want it in the house."

Clara rose, jaw tight. "Show us."

He did. And sure enough, beneath the ceramic pot, nestled in a bed of damp moss, was the envelope. Inside: ten crisp twenty-dollar bills and a folded slip of paper in Pike's unmistakable handwriting: Silence is a gardener's virtue. Discretion will be rewarded.

Back at the inn, the envelope lay open between them on the parlor table. Clara stared at the note, the script neat and cruel.

"Subtlety isn't exactly his strength," Amelia muttered.

Clara's reply was measured. "No. But audacity is."

She pulled out her notebook and began to sketch a timeline. Melvin's confession fit snugly into a sequence that was becoming harder and harder for Pike to deny.

That afternoon, Clara made her way to Gossamer Fables. She needed clarity—the kind only paper and Mr. Lark's sage calm could offer.

Mr. Lark looked up from a stack of gardening almanacs as she entered. "Afternoon, Clara. You look like a woman on the brink of toppling an empire."

"Getting closer," she replied. She explained everything.

He listened without interruption, then led her to a back shelf.

"Green binder. Top left. The garden committee minutes from the 1980s. Annette Farnsworth was a regular contributor. You may find something familiar."

She opened it at the worktable. Inside were yellowed letters, committee minutes, and clippings. One in particular caught her breath—a letter from Annette protesting development near the ridge, citing land preservation and heritage.

Clara photographed the pages, her pulse quickening. "This isn't new. Pike is continuing a decades-long effort."

Back at the inn, she spread the evidence on the table like a general plotting a counterstrike. Documents. Photos. The bribe. The note. A growing wall of truth against a fortress of deceit.

Amelia entered with fresh tea. "We present this tomorrow. To the mayor. No more side doors."

Clara nodded. "Agreed. It's time to pull this into the light."

Lady Grey entered then, her fur gleaming in the golden light, and leapt lightly onto the bench beside Clara. Her amber eyes blinked slowly, knowingly.

Clara scratched behind her ears. "Another piece in place, little one."

Outside, dusk softened the town, but the hush was different now. Not fearful. Focused. And within the walls of the Tumblebrook Inn, history no longer whispered from hidden ledgers and buried boxes.

It shouted.

And someone was finally listening.

Chapter 35

The Attic Intruder

The storm arrived in earnest just past midnight, rattling the very bones of the Tumblebrook Inn. Rain lashed the windows in furious bursts, like nature's own percussion pounding out a war rhythm. Lightning forked across the sky, illuminating the lake in ghostly flashes, and thunder followed with groaning rumblings that made the rafters tremble. The inn creaked and moaned in reply, as though it too bore witness to something unseen. But tonight, something in the rafters felt different—not just creaky and old, but watchful.

Most of the inn's guests were asleep, curled under quilts and unaware of the secrets shifting just above their heads. But Lady Grey was not among them.

From her perch on the windowsill in Amelia's bedroom, the sleek British Shorthair watched the rain streak the glass. Her amber eyes glinted with restless energy. Something stirred beyond the storm—something more than wind or rain. Her tail twitched, then thudded once against the sill, her instincts prickling like fine needles.

She leapt silently to the floor, moving like liquid shadow through the hallway. Up one flight, then another, each step placed with feline precision. She reached the narrow stretch near the attic and paused. The ceiling sloped more steeply here, the hallway narrowing to an old, arched door with a tarnished handle and peeling paint.

The draft beneath the door carried a medley of scents—dust, cedarwood, mothballs, and faint traces of something newer. Ink. Maybe even cologne. That, more than anything, made her ears perk. She paused, nose twitching. The faint cologne matched the one she'd sniffed on the hydrangea path the night she vanished. Her memory, sharper than most humans', cataloged the scent like a library tag—danger, page one.

Lady Grey reared on her hind legs, balancing gracefully, and tapped at the latch. It had been left slightly ajar since Amelia's last search through her great-aunt Annie's old things. The cat's delicate paw eased it open further with a soft creak.

She slipped into the dark.

The attic smelled of time and memory—quilted cedar trunks, paper and glue, faded linen, and forgotten perfume. Boxes towered in uneven stacks, some labeled in Amelia's tidy handwriting: "Festival Records," "Holiday Trinkets," "Annie's Correspondence."

But amid the archival clutter sat something out of place.

A modern plastic bin, dark gray and conspicuously new, its glossy sides gleaming in the errant flash of lightning. Unlike the other containers, it bore no label. It was shoved behind an old wooden coat rack and partially hidden under a moth-eaten wool shawl.

Lady Grey crept closer. The bin's scent was sterile, sharp—rubber, paper, and vinyl. A curious, electric tang clung to it. Her instincts sharpened. This was not Amelia's handiwork.

With a calculating twitch of her whiskers, she circled the bin, testing its weight with a cautious paw. The lid held steady. Another paw, this one more forceful. The lid shifted, then popped free with a soft clunk, tipping askew.

Papers cascaded like snow.

Lady Grey jumped back and landed in a crouch. When nothing

stirred, she inched forward again. Scattered around her were documents—blueprints, printed emails, highlighted land survey maps, and typed notes full of aggressive zoning language. There was more than permits and maps. A printed email titled "Preliminary Ridge Subdivision – Q3 Acquisition Plan" outlined Phase III: vacation buyouts. Dozens of lots. The plan wasn't just to take the inn—it was to absorb the town.

At the center was a handwritten phrase on torn notebook paper:

"Initiate Phase II: Ridge acquisition, expedited. Cover with rezoning."

Lady Grey sniffed the paper, then used a paw to turn it over. More documents lay beneath, one bearing the distinct letterhead of the Tumblebrook Council and another with Vincent Pike's signature beside a company logo Clara had circled in her notebook earlier that week.

The evidence was damning. And all of it hidden right above their heads.

She froze. Her ears perked.

Footsteps. Slow and deliberate, muffled by the storm—but close.

Lady Grey dove for cover beneath a stack of vintage bed frames draped in crochet throws. The attic door creaked wide. A flashlight beam knifed through the dark, followed by slow, deliberate steps. Vincent Pike stepped in, shoulders tight, eyes sweeping the room with practiced precision.

"Someone's been here," he muttered—not to himself, but like a warning to the shadows.

His flashlight beam landed on the toppled bin. He hissed in frustration and dropped to his knees, shoving papers back into the container with quick, frantic motions.

He missed a page.

It fluttered just beyond his reach, wedged beneath a framed photograph of the inn circa 1910. On it, a blueprint of the Tumblebrook Inn's grounds bore a red X scrawled on the northeast corner. He didn't see it. But Lady Grey did.

When he left, taking the bin with him, thinking he had fully closed the attic behind him, she waited until the floorboards stilled. Then she emerged.

She sniffed the air, confirmed he was gone, and padded over to the overlooked paper. Her claws tapped once against the floor as she hooked the edge. With careful nudging and a practiced flick of her paw, she dragged it toward the attic's single window, where moonlight had returned.

She studied the paper. The red X bisected an old outline labeled "Root Cellar Access Tunnel." The label was faded, but Clara had seen it before—in Annie's notes, under the words: "First they take what's beneath, then what's above."

Lady Grey didn't understand blueprints. But she understood secrets. And she understood the importance of returning it to those who could act.

Clutching the page gently in her teeth, she trotted down the attic steps. She avoided the creaky stair and slipped into Clara's room through the cracked door.

The young woman stirred in bed as Lady Grey leapt up beside her and dropped the paper on her chest.

Clara blinked. "Lady...?"

She picked up the sheet and gasped. "Amelia!"

Moments later, the two women were seated side-by-side, the blueprint spread between them.

"That X—" Clara whispered.

"That's near the root cellar," Amelia said. "Just beyond the herb garden. But why would Vincent—?"

Lady Grey hopped down and padded to the door, tail flicking with impatient authority.

Clara looked at her. "You want us to follow?"

Thunder rolled again outside. But something in the storm had already shifted.

"Let's go," Amelia said. "Now."

They grabbed boots and coats, flashlights and umbrellas. Lady Grey led the way, a silver blur darting ahead of their lamplight.

Behind them, the attic returned to its silence. But a truth once uncovered can never again be hidden.

And thanks to Lady Grey, the secrets buried at the northeast corner of Tumblebrook Inn were one step closer to the light.

Chapter 36

Disgraced Official

Rain misted gently over Tumblebrook the morning Amelia set out to verify the newest—and perhaps most damning—piece of the puzzle. The hush over the inn felt different—less the quietude of peace and more the held breath of anticipation. As she moved through the foyer, the scent of orange peel polish and lavender drifted through the air. It was almost enough to make her forget the secrets hanging just above the town like storm clouds.

Clara had gone to the bookshop to double-check property records again, and Lady Grey had curled up by the fireplace, still weary from the stormy attic encounter. That left Amelia to face the town planner, Harold Kemper, on her own.

Harold's office occupied a modest annex at the far end of town hall. Amelia had called ahead and pretended it was a routine festival follow-up. In truth, her palms hadn't stopped sweating since she'd made the appointment. Tucked into her bag were photocopies of damning blueprints, zoning forms, and the annotated note marked "Initiate Phase II: Ridge acquisition."

She arrived ten minutes early. The hallway outside Harold's door smelled of dry wood and old coffee. A flickering lightbulb above the filing cabinet buzzed ominously, casting a jittery energy through the corridor. The narrow space reminded her of the stacks at Gossamer Fables, though with far less charm and far more bureaucratic burden.

She knocked.

"Come in!" Harold's chipper voice called.

The door creaked open to reveal a small, cluttered office. Certificates of planning expertise lined the walls beside smiling photos of Harold with mayors past and present. He stood when she entered, his sweater vest snug and his hair meticulously combed, though his eyes darted more than she remembered.

"Amelia Farnsworth! I heard the garden festival went beautifully," he said with rehearsed cheer. "What can I do for the innkeeper of the hour?"

She smiled, polite but tight. "It's about the zoning forms. I had some... questions."

His brow twitched ever so slightly. "Of course, of course. Why don't you have a seat?"

She lowered herself into the chair across from his desk and placed her bag on her lap. "I was looking through my great-aunt Annie's old documents. You know how detailed she was with land records. She left me some older surveys. In comparing them to the current zoning... something didn't add up."

Harold cleared his throat. "Well, zoning can be confusing—changes happen over time, especially when land usage evolves. A flower bed here, a shed there. It's all standard procedure."

She gave a slow nod, then pulled out the first document—one of the official blueprints stamped with his name. "This document says the ridge was rezoned last year, but there's no notation in the town's public minutes. Nor is there a signature from the council."

He frowned, adjusting his glasses. "That could be a filing error. It happens more often than you'd think."

"Except it's not just one error," she said, sliding more papers across the desk. "It's a pattern. These forms—two of them—bear your signature and the stamp of the council. But according to Clara's review, the stamp doesn't match the one currently in use."

Harold's smile faltered. "You've been... cross-referencing council stamps?"

"I've been investigating a missing cat, Harold," she said, her voice gentle but steady. "But now I'm looking at land fraud, forged documents, and potentially illegal rezoning that benefits only one man—Vincent Pike."

The planner's hands trembled slightly as he reached for a tissue. "Amelia, listen, I—I didn't want to be involved. He pressured me. Said it was harmless. Just smoothing out boundaries. No one was going to lose anything."

"But they were. The inn's land. And Clara found one deed removed from the bookshop's archives. Someone's tried to erase our history."

He slumped into his chair. "He said it was already approved. That the council would retroactively approve it. He paid me to stamp the papers early. Just once. Then another favor. It spiraled."

Amelia stared, stunned. "He bribed you."

"He said it wasn't a bribe. That it was just encouragement. That this kind of thing happens in every small town. I—" Harold's voice cracked. "I've made a mistake, Amelia."

She sat back, torn between anger and pity. "Then help me fix it."

"I can't undo the forms now. But I can give you the originals. The real ones. The unaltered maps. They're in my locked drawer."

He bent and retrieved a narrow folio. Inside were hand-drawn plats, initialed by Annie Farnsworth, with the inn's boundaries clearly intact—including the disputed ridge.

"They were never meant to be rezoned," he said. "It's your land."

She took the folder reverently. "You'll need to come forward. Tell the council what happened."

"I'll draft a full statement. And I'll resign."

The weight of his words lingered in the room like smoke. Amelia stood and extended her hand. "Thank you, Harold."

He shook it, eyes glassy. "Tell Annie I'm sorry."

"I think she'd forgive you."

As Amelia stepped out into the street, the mist had lifted. The rooftops of Tumblebrook gleamed, washed clean by the rain, catching slivers of early sunlight. She paused outside the annex, breathing in the scent of damp earth and tulips blooming stubbornly beside the walkway. Her heart pounded—not with fear, but with resolve.

She headed straight for the inn, her boots splashing through shallow puddles as the clouds slowly broke overhead. She could already picture Clara at the kitchen table, a mug of tea in hand and Lady Grey nestled at her feet. They had faced secrets, storms, and shadows. But now, they held something powerful—the truth.

That truth, inscribed in ink and sealed in signatures, was finally in their hands.

And soon, the entire town of Tumblebrook would know it.

Chapter 37

Connecting the Conspiracy

Tumblebrook awoke to one of those cloud-streaked mornings that smelled like history—earthy, humid, and humming with untold truths. Clara Henderson sat in her usual corner of Gossamer Fables, the bookstore not yet open to the public. Her mug of chamomile tea cooled beside a half-eaten blueberry scone. Around her sprawled a collage of papers, maps, ledger fragments, zoning applications, and photocopied deeds, each marked with bright sticky tabs and annotations in her looping script.

She had spent the night combing through everything they'd uncovered—every blueprint, deed fragment, journal entry, newspaper clipping, and township file. Her eyes were sore and her neck ached from hunching over the table, but sleep was an afterthought. The deeper she dug, the clearer it became: the land grab targeting the inn wasn't new. It was the final phase of a conspiracy that had wound its way through decades, cloaked in civic charm and community rituals.

Lady Grey sat poised on the counter, tail flicking in sync with the shop's antique clock. Clara tapped her pencil against the notebook's edge. "It's not just about Vincent," she murmured to the cat. "This whole thing has roots older than both of us."

The turning point had been Amelia's great-aunt Annie's journal, found behind a false wall in the inn. Its veiled references to clandestine meetings, coded notes about "preserving the ridge," and mentions of a secretive group had once seemed like eccentric musings. But in light of the altered blueprints, falsified deeds, and the Monarch Society's resurging symbol, the truth was impossible to deny.

Clara unfurled a roll of butcher paper across the table and began constructing a timeline. She anchored it with Annie's first mention of the Monarch Society in 1971—a group originally formed to safeguard Tumblebrook's architectural integrity. But over time, their mission had warped. Preservation became pretext. Acquisition replaced stewardship.

She circled a cluster of land sales in the late 1980s. Adjacent lots changed hands through shell companies, the owners veiled behind vague addresses and foreign names. The inn, however, remained untouched—protected by Annie's unusually worded trust deed barring third-party claims without familial consent.

Next came the Garden Festival in the early '90s—a celebration Clara now recognized as strategic theater. It had been launched just months before a zoning permit subtly redefined the ridge boundary near the inn. A seemingly innocent community event had masked a quiet land grab.

"All smoke and roses," Clara muttered. "The festival was the misdirection."

The bell above the shop door jingled. Amelia stepped in, her coat damp with morning mist, clutching a thick envelope bearing the town seal.

"Harold's confession," she said. "Signed and notarized. He's resigning. And the council's calling an emergency session tomorrow."

Clara stood to greet her. "That's incredible. We might actually get some justice."

They sat at the timeline table. Clara gestured to a marked point in 2002. "Here's where the next move happened—a resolution to expand zoning around the ridge for a 'wellness facility.' It failed by one vote. Guess who drafted it?"

"Harold?"

Clara nodded grimly. "But back then, he worked for Monarch Holdings. Different name, same symbol. The butterfly insignia matches what we found in Annie's journal."

"They rebranded," Amelia said. "Shifted from heritage protectors to profiteers."

"And the inn was their missing puzzle piece. Annie's deed blocked every attempt. That's why she left the journal. That's why she stayed so private."

Lady Grey trilled softly and leapt from the counter, prowling toward a dust-heavy cabinet.

"What about Vincent's mysterious developer friend?" Amelia asked.

Clara slid over a folder labeled LEASE INTENT. "Still no name, but he represents a firm tied to something called a 'heritage innovation corridor.' Sounds noble, but the company has leveled three historic inns in other states and replaced them with boutique condos."

She unrolled an updated zoning map. "This was going to be filed next month. The ridge's boundary? Gone."

"We were weeks from losing everything," Amelia said.

They worked well into the afternoon. Clara condensed the evidence into a presentation. Amelia drafted a narrative summary of their findings. They included:

- Vincent's redlined zoning map
- Harold's confession
- A photograph comparing the forged and authentic council stamps
- A printed rezoning order with an incomplete timestamp
- Emails between Vincent and Monarch Holdings

- Annie's original trust deed with annotations

Clara added a scanned letter from 1979 in Annie's hand: *Beware cultivated friendships that serve profit over heritage. Tumblebrook must remain whole.*

They affixed it to the end of the timeline—a final word from the past.

Just before dusk, Doris sent over pastries and a thermos of cocoa. "From the café," the delivery girl said. "She said not to let truth go underfed."

By twilight, the timeline stretched across tables and shelves, color-coded and carefully mounted. Clara took photos and sent one to Mr. Lark.

His reply came within minutes: *You've unearthed the root. Water it with justice.*

Outside, the ridge loomed—no longer just a line on a map but a symbol. Inside, two women and a cat had transformed the town's buried truth into something undeniable.

Tomorrow, Tumblebrook would hear it.

Chapter 38

The Trap is Set

Tumblebrook's morning arrived dressed in its Sunday best— soft golden light spilling over dew-speckled rooftops, bird-song trilling like orchestral warmups, and the comforting clatter of café dishes drifting from Doris Finch's open-air kitchen. From the porch of the Tumblebrook Inn, Amelia Farnsworth surveyed the town with a mixture of fondness and fierce determination. This was her home, her legacy—and today, it was her stage.

The town appreciation event was a fabrication, of course. There were no commemorative speeches or golden plaques, no historical milestones to honor. But it looked convincing enough: banners fluttered in the breeze bearing phrases like "Tumblebrook: Where Roots Run Deep" and "A Garden of Thanks." Tables had been set up in the square, filled with pastries, tea, lemonade, and Doris's best tomato tarts. Floral arrangements ringed the gazebo in a swirl of spring color. If deception was a performance, Amelia was delivering a show worthy of a standing ovation.

Lady Grey wound herself around Amelia's ankles, purring softly, then bounded up onto the bannister to bask in the sun. Clara, note-book in hand, approached from the garden path.

"He confirmed he's coming," Clara said. "Said he wouldn't miss 'a celebration of this caliber.'"

Amelia raised an eyebrow. "Arrogant, isn't he?"

Clara grinned. "It's his one consistent trait."

Inside, the inn had been transformed. The lobby featured fresh bouquets, subtle stacks of records, and an innocuous binder on the counter containing the entire timeline Clara had built—a quiet trap in plain sight.

"It needs to look like an accident if he sees it," Amelia said. "As if a curious guest stumbled onto it."

"We're setting bait, not writing a novel," Clara replied. "But yes, subtle."

They reviewed the plan. Vincent Pike would arrive before lunch. Officer Wexley, in plain clothes, would intercept him with a casual zoning question—just enough to bait a careless admission. Meanwhile, Amelia and Clara would be ready to tip the council and publicly reveal everything if Vincent took the bait.

"Doris is placing him at the garden table with the strongest lemonade and the weakest shade," Clara said, tapping her notes. "That should keep him sweating."

"And Mr. Lark?"

"Stationed in the gazebo with a copy of the Monarch archive, just waiting to be noticed."

Lady Grey pawed at a crate near the fireplace. Inside were Annie's journal and the rusted lockbox of old deeds.

"You found the truth before we did," Amelia murmured, stroking her fur. "Now let's see if the town is ready to hear it."

By noon, the square hummed with cautious festivity. Townsfolk sipped cider and wandered between flower stands. Children raced through the hedge maze. Clara had ensured the event felt light-hearted—so no one would suspect the confrontation it was designed to contain.

Vincent Pike arrived in a pressed blazer and sunglasses, walking like a man certain the world still belonged to him.

"Amelia," he said, removing his glasses. "You outdo yourself."

"We like to celebrate what matters," Amelia said.

"Indeed. Small towns are about tradition. Speaking of which..." He produced a folded letter from his inner pocket. "Just a draft of an investment proposal. Vision requires courage."

Amelia accepted the letter with a measured smile. "I'll give it a read."

Clara appeared beside her. "And history requires truth. Hope you find both today."

Vincent offered a patronizing smile and turned to mingle.

Meanwhile, Officer Wexley approached. "Mr. Pike?"

Vincent turned. "Ah, law enforcement. Shouldn't you be directing traffic?"

Wexley held firm. "A piece of mail was misdelivered. Zoning paperwork. Pretty substantial."

Vincent hesitated. "A misunderstanding. My developer friend must've gotten ahead of the paperwork."

"Developer friend?"

"Just a turn of phrase. Speculative real estate. You know how it is."

In the gazebo, Mr. Lark discreetly snapped a photo and texted it to Clara.

Amelia tapped a spoon to her cider glass. "May I have your attention?"

The square quieted. Lady Grey took position on the podium steps.

"Today isn't just about flowers or history," Amelia said. "It's about what we protect."

Clara unrolled the timeline onto an easel.

"Our investigation uncovered forged documents, manipulated boundaries, and a decades-long plan to absorb the inn through dishonest zoning," Clara said.

Gasps rippled through the crowd.

Vincent stepped forward. "I don't know what you're insinuating."

Amelia held up an evidence bag. "We found this in your shed. A map. A lock of gray fur."

Vincent paled. "That proves nothing. Cats wander."

"But your attic told a different story," Clara said. "And your connection to Monarch Holdings ties it all together."

Wexley stepped forward. "Mr. Pike, I need you to come with me."

The crowd murmured as Vincent blustered, but the trap had sprung.

That evening, under the soft glow of porch lanterns, Amelia and Clara sat in silence.

"We did it," Clara whispered.

"We protected what matters," Amelia replied.

Lady Grey leapt into Amelia's lap, purring like the exhale of a secret finally spoken.

Tumblebrook would heal. And it would remember.

Chapter 39

Vanished Again

Tumblebrook awoke to a silvery mist that clung to the trees like cobwebs, wrapping each budding branch and painted storefront in eerie stillness. It was the sort of morning that felt suspended in time, thick with the weight of anticipation—the kind of atmosphere that whispered secrets through the breeze and nudged old stories to the surface. Clara stood by the bookshop's front window, her hands cupped around a chipped mug of coffee. Beyond the glass, the town square gradually stirred to life. Garden banners still fluttered from the festival, but their vibrant cheer felt hollow today. Something had shifted.

The trap they'd set had worked. Vincent Pike had been cornered, exposed—not just for land scheming, but for orchestrating deception deep into the town's roots. And yet, despite that victory, Clara couldn't shake the feeling that something remained unfinished. A hollow space between facts. An echo that hadn't quite faded.

She turned away from the fogged window and glanced down at her notebook sprawled across the counter. Lines of ink crisscrossed its pages like spiderwebs: names, dates, maps, forged documents, property surveys. They had uncovered nearly every strand of the conspiracy. Almost.

The bell above the shop door jingled softly. Clara looked up to see Amelia step inside, her scarf damp with fog and her green eyes tired, laced with urgency.

"He's gone," Amelia said simply, her voice low.

Clara's stomach dropped. "Gone?"

"Didn't show for the hearing. Officer Wexley went to check on him. His car's still running."

"In town?"

"No. Trailhead. North Woods."

Of course. If someone wanted to disappear—or be disappeared—there was no better place.

They reached the edge of the North Woods in under twenty minutes. Amelia drove, the tires humming anxiously beneath them, while Clara sat rigid in the passenger seat, gripping her notebook like it might shatter. Officer Wexley's cruiser was already parked near the trail, quiet and watchful. The air smelled of wet moss and pine, the scent thick with rain-soaked memory.

Vincent's silver sedan sat idle nearby, its front door swung wide open. A faint buzzing sound came from the still-running engine. Clara approached carefully. Inside, the leather seats were pristine. On the passenger seat: a closed briefcase. No wallet. No phone. Just the faintest trace of cologne and an unsettling silence.

"Keys are in the ignition," Wexley said as he joined them. "His wallet's in the glove compartment. Nothing's disturbed."

"He didn't take anything?" Amelia asked, frowning.

Wexley shook his head. "Makes no sense."

Clara's gaze swept across the clearing. "Unless he wasn't planning to leave. Or he left in a hurry... or not of his own will."

Wexley glanced around, his hand twitching near his belt. "The trail's mostly undisturbed, except for one set of prints. Leading north."

"Let me guess," Clara murmured. "One set going in. None coming out."

* * *

Lady Grey had insisted on coming. The sleek British Shorthair darted into the woods ahead of them, her steps silent, her amber eyes alert. She moved with uncanny certainty, pausing at intervals to glance back and guide them forward.

The deeper they went, the more the forest wrapped around them. Branches tangled overhead. The trail narrowed until it was barely more than an animal path. Then Clara stopped.

"There." She pointed to an indentation in the dirt. "Fresh. Drag marks, too."

They followed the signs through a thicket of bramble and fallen birch. A hollow came into view, and nestled within it—a small, rotting structure.

"The forester's shack," Clara murmured.

Amelia frowned. "That was supposed to be condemned."

They approached slowly. The door creaked open at the lightest touch. Inside was a single room: lantern, shelf, crate-table, and a few moldy food cans. But on the back wall hung something unmistakable.

A map. And next to it, pages tacked to the wood.

"Printouts," Clara whispered. "Emails."

She read quickly. "From Monarch Holdings. Addressed to Vincent Pike."

"Why would he leave these here?" Amelia asked.

"Unless he didn't," Clara said. "Unless someone else wanted us to find them."

She plucked one page down and examined the email string— zoning amendments, compensation plans, and veiled language about public obfuscation. Names were redacted, but the tone was clear:

these weren't civic plans. They were acquisitions dressed in noble intentions.

Wexley stepped inside, his brows furrowed. "This place was empty yesterday. I passed by doing trail checks."

"So someone planted these," Clara said. "It's a message."

"Or a warning," Amelia added.

* * *

By late afternoon, the news had spread.

Vincent Pike had vanished. Some said it was shame. Others swore he had faked it all and fled. A few whispered of retribution from unseen forces—perhaps even from within Monarch's inner ring. By dusk, the town square had become a cluster of hushed theories.

At the inn, guests clutched cups of tea and offered sympathetic looks. But it was Lady Grey's behavior that spoke loudest. She paced the windowsill, ears twitching at every sound from the woods.

Clara and Amelia returned to the study, pulling out everything they'd collected—journals, maps, letters, property ledgers. They spread it across the table like a jigsaw puzzle with too many pieces missing. But now they knew where to look.

Lady Grey leapt onto the table and stared at the map.

She pawed at a spot.

"The ridgeline," Clara said.

Amelia leaned closer. There, barely visible beneath the topographic lines, was the Monarch Society's symbol—faint but unmistakable.

"Not just a mark," Clara said. "It's their signature. Their next move."

Lady Grey gave a low trill.

"They're not done," Amelia murmured. "Even without Vincent."

Clara nodded slowly. "Then we'll be ready."

Chapter 40

Trail of Paper

The storm had passed, but the sky above Tumblebrook still bore its bruises—lavender-gray streaks stained with reluctant sunlight. Amelia Farnsworth stood on the wraparound porch of the Tumblebrook Inn, her gaze trailing beyond the edge of the garden to where the forest loomed. Somewhere in those trees, hidden beneath roots of corruption and tangled secrets, lay the truth about the land—and the forces determined to seize it.

She clutched the latest piece of evidence—a torn corner of a topographic map Lady Grey had unearthed from beneath the cedar wardrobe in Room Three. The handwriting in the margin matched what they'd seen before: precise, slanted, unmistakably Vincent Pike's. But what stood out wasn't just the coordinates. It was the faint Monarch Society insignia, stamped in silver wax at the bottom.

Clara emerged from the inn's entryway, notebook in hand, eyes sharp with caffeinated determination. "The coordinates match the south slope. Past the ridge. I cross-referenced them with the county land office's archives."

Amelia raised a brow. "And?"

"There's a service path that runs just behind the inn. Not on any public surveys. Probably part of the old Monarch delivery network."

Lady Grey padded between them, tail flicking with impatient authority, as if to say: Let's go already.

The service path was overgrown with early spring growth, blackberry brambles curling toward the trail like skeletal hands. The farther they walked, the more the inn felt like part of another world. The trees thickened, the air dampened. A hush fell over the trail, muffling their footfalls as if nature itself were holding its breath.

Half a mile in, they found it: a rusted iron gate hanging on bent hinges, barely visible behind a row of crumbling hedges. Clara pulled a pair of gloves from her coat pocket and shoved it open with a groan.

Beyond stood a low, narrow structure of faux-painted concrete. Not the developer's office on Main Street—this one bore a brass plaque: North Star Land Group – Field Records Unit B.

"I've never heard of them," Amelia said.

Clara flipped open her notebook. "That's because they're a Monarch Holdings subsidiary. Disguised through six shell companies. Pike referenced it in his ledger."

They tried the door. Locked.

"Standard latch," Clara said, kneeling beside the knob. "Keep watch?"

Amelia nodded, casting glances over her shoulder. Lady Grey sniffed the doorframe, then sat with regal stillness.

A click. The door creaked open.

Inside, the air reeked of damp paper and cheap toner. Rows of filing cabinets lined the walls. A map of Tumblebrook hung on a corkboard in the corner, full of overlapping boundaries and color-coded circles.

Clara's eyes narrowed. "They plotted every parcel around the inn. Look—these red dots mark negotiation targets."

Amelia pointed. "And this one—" she traced a faded line—"that's our fence line."

Clara yanked open a cabinet drawer. "Acquisition plans. All

dated after Pike bought in. They've been buying land under different names."

Amelia stepped to a dusty credenza where a locked binder sat beneath a cracked lamp. She flipped it open.

Inside: photographs. Surveillance shots of Amelia, Clara, the inn, the bookshop—even Lady Grey sunbathing on the porch.

"They were watching us the whole time."

As the sun dipped behind the trees, the documents began forming a timeline. Clara arranged them on a drafting table while Amelia snapped photos with her phone.

One page caught Amelia's eye—a memorandum from an unnamed executive to Vincent:

Ensure town sentiment is controlled. Focus on acquisition through indirect influence. Use Festival permits as leverage.

Below that: a note in Vincent's hand.

Resistance: C. Henderson and A. Farnsworth. Cat = asset?

Amelia read it twice.

"Asset?" Clara scoffed. "What on earth does that mean?"

"Maybe they thought Lady Grey had... value. Or leverage."

Lady Grey growled softly. She padded to a slightly ajar drawer, nudging it open. Inside: architectural sketches of the inn—crawlspaces, attic panels, foundation vents.

"They were planning an entry," Clara whispered. "Not just observation."

Amelia's mouth went dry. "They were going to take something. Or someone."

Hours passed in silent fury. By the time they emerged, dusk had fallen. The first stars blinked to life above the ridgeline. Amelia carried a box of documents. Clara had the office's only functioning hard drive.

They didn't speak until they were back on the trail.

"They built this whole plan on lies," Clara said finally. "Falsified deeds. Bribed officials. Manipulated records. And they almost got away with it."

"If not for a missing cat," Amelia said, managing a bitter smile.

Lady Grey flicked her tail in dignified acknowledgment.

Back at the inn, they spread everything across the dining table.

Ezra arrived first, summoned by Clara's cryptic message. Then Doris from the café, bearing a pie like an offering. Mr. Lark followed, clutching three leather-bound journals he claimed would clarify Monarch rituals.

Amelia gestured to the map. "This is what we found. A takeover decades in the making. Disguised as civic development. All connected to Vincent Pike—and whoever still controls Monarch Holdings."

Ezra pointed to the ledger. "This handwriting matches the mural grant application. That 'anonymous donor' wasn't charitable."

"Do we go public?" Clara asked.

"Not yet," Amelia said. "We need the full chain of proof. Not just papers. We need someone inside Monarch Holdings."

As if on cue, Lady Grey leapt onto the table and pawed a page Amelia hadn't noticed.

A fax cover sheet. Barely legible.

To: H.C., Monarch Holdings, Field Unit B. Re: Phase Two Acquisition Schedule

"H.C.," Amelia murmured. "Who is that?"

"Not Vincent," Clara said. "He wasn't in charge. Just a pawn."

"No," Amelia said, a cold clarity settling in. "This goes further. And we just opened the wrong door."

Lady Grey let out a long, deliberate meow.

The chase wasn't over. It had just entered its most dangerous stretch.

<h1 style="text-align:center">Chapter 41</h1>

<h2 style="text-align:center">Final Clue</h2>

Lady Grey leapt onto the windowsill of the developer's temporary office, her paw pads silent against the cool glass as she peered into the dimly lit interior. The rain had finally ceased, leaving behind a damp hush and the scent of wet earth and pine. Her amber eyes narrowed. There it was again—that scent of varnish and old paper, the same one that had clung to Vincent's clothes the day he arrived in Tumblebrook.

The office had been hastily assembled in the developer's cottage, a once-cozy structure now stripped of charm and repurposed into a nerve center of scheming. The walls were lined with shelves of blueprints, labeled folders, and detailed survey charts. But Lady Grey's attention was on a battered oak desk near the far wall. Something about it felt... unfinished. Her whiskers twitched. The air around it felt heavier, like secrets had sunk into the very grain of the wood.

She padded soundlessly through the cracked-open door. No one was inside. The storm had likely driven the occupants away—or they assumed no one would dare snoop on such a dreary afternoon. Their mistake.

The desk drawers were all closed, but Lady Grey knew better

than to take things at face value. She jumped lightly onto the chair, then onto the desk itself. The surface was strewn with architectural sketches, meeting notes, a laptop powered down, and a half-drunk cup of stale coffee. Her tail swished once. With practiced precision, she slid her paw behind one of the side drawers.

Something resisted.

She clawed delicately but persistently at the inner corner. Wood creaked. A faint shudder. Then—clunk.

The bottom drawer lurched forward an inch, revealing a false panel that shifted when nudged. Behind it was a thin envelope, its edges yellowed, its seal broken. Lady Grey hooked a claw beneath it and dragged it into the open.

Inside was a folded letter.

Amelia's scent lingered on the doorframe. Good. She was near.

Amelia had only stepped outside to check on the rain gutters when she saw Lady Grey dart from the cottage toward her, eyes gleaming and a letter grasped delicately in her teeth.

"What have you got there, darling?" she murmured, kneeling down. Lady Grey dropped the envelope at her feet.

Amelia's heart thudded.

She recognized the handwriting instantly. Great-Aunt Annie's.

She opened the envelope with shaking fingers. Inside was a single sheet of parchment and a notarized statement:

I, Annabelle Farnsworth, witnessed a private agreement between members of the Monarch Society and Lawrence Pike in 1973 to alter land surveys and secure future development rights under false pretenses. The inn's northern boundary was redrawn without disclosure. I've kept copies. They are buried beneath the hearthstone.

Amelia gasped. "Clara!"

Within minutes, Clara arrived, breathless, her boots splashed with mud. She took one look at the letter and paled.

"This is it," she whispered. "This is what ties it all together. This is what they were hiding."

They hurried to the inn, Lady Grey in the lead, tail held high like a triumphant banner. In the sitting room, they moved aside the hearth rug and pried loose the corner stone. Beneath it lay a metal box.

Inside: copies of deeds, annotated blueprints, and—most damning of all—a signed confession from the town planner who had recently resigned in disgrace.

"He knew," Clara said. "And so did Vincent. They just didn't think anyone would ever find this."

Amelia sat back on her heels, tears springing to her eyes. "Annie tried to protect us. Even after all these years. She knew this day might come."

Lady Grey, now curled contentedly on the rug, gave a satisfied meow and began grooming her paw.

The town meeting was hastily called. By dusk, the inn's ballroom was filled to capacity. Town council members, shopkeepers, festival volunteers—everyone was there. The heavy scent of anticipation clung to the air.

Amelia stood at the front, the metal box at her side, Clara beside her. Her voice shook only once as she began.

"This town deserves to know the truth," Amelia said. "And thanks to those who never stopped believing in it, the truth has come home."

She read from the confession. Clara displayed the forged blueprints, the false boundary surveys, and the notarized statement from Annabelle Farnsworth. Gasps rippled through the crowd like wind across water.

Lady Grey, perched regally on the presentation table, watched as a wave of realization spread across the townsfolk.

Doris from the café gasped aloud and clutched the hand of her husband, Harold. "I knew there was something wrong," she whispered. "But this...this is betrayal."

Mr. Lark removed his glasses and began to weep quietly, his voice a hushed rasp. "I gave them trust. I gave them history. And they took it all to build lies."

Eleanor Vance clutched her pearls and stepped forward. "My family's land was part of that original sale. They told us it was for a community garden. And I believed them."

A rising tide of voices followed—questions, accusations, tearful acknowledgments. Some residents embraced in disbelief, others shook their heads, overwhelmed by the sheer scale of what had been hidden from them.

Even Officer Wexley, who had stumbled so often in the investigation, looked deeply moved. "I'll have this submitted to the state auditor by morning," he said hoarsely. "And I'll be reopening the case files tied to any suspicious property transfers."

Mayor Tom Keegan stood slowly from his chair, his expression stern. "There will be a full public inquiry. No more secrets. No more whispered meetings in back rooms. If this town is to have a future, it begins now—with truth."

But it was the silence afterward that said everything.

The weight of history. The resolve for change. The final acknowledgment of betrayal—and the first steps toward healing.

That night, the inn was quieter than it had been in weeks. The wind outside was calm. The lake was still, its surface mirror-like under the moon's glow.

Lady Grey sat in the window of Amelia's bedroom, her tail curling slowly as she looked out over the moonlit trees.

She had done what needed to be done.

She had uncovered the final clue.

The past had been illuminated, and Tumblebrook had found its voice again.

But something in the distance still called to her.

Beyond the ridge, beyond the whispers, a new mystery waited.

And when it was ready, she'd find it.

After all, some cats were born to guard more than hearth and home. Some guarded history. And some, like Lady Grey, guarded truth.

Epilogue

New Roots

The first days of summer arrived gently in Tumblebrook, carried on a breeze scented with lilacs, lemon balm, and freshly mown grass. The lake shimmered beneath a flawless sky—no longer concealing secrets, but reflecting the quiet strength of a town that had faced them all—and endured.

Amelia Farnsworth stood on the porch of the Tumblebrook Inn, one hand wrapped around a cool glass of iced tea, the other resting on the bannister where ivy now crept freely. No longer trimmed back in fear of bulldozers or forged claims, it was allowed to grow—wild, determined, and honest. Much like the town itself.

Behind her, the inn hummed with familiar life. Luggage wheels clattered against hardwood floors. Clara's laughter floated from the kitchen, where she was testing a new peach-cardamom bundt cake recipe. A guest asked for directions to the lakeside labyrinth.

Lady Grey, of course, was exactly where she belonged: sprawled across the railing in a shaft of sunlight, amber eyes half-lidded in serene satisfaction. Since the truth had come out, she'd become something of a local legend—Tumblebrook's patron saint of mystery and mischief. There was even talk—mostly from Doris—of commissioning a statue: mid-leap, paw raised in defiance. Lady Grey, ever above such pageantry, had declined all public appearances and continued her silent vigil.

"Can you believe it?" Clara emerged onto the porch, brushing flour from her apron. "We actually saved the inn. And half the town, really."

Amelia watched a pair of children race down the lake path, butterfly nets clutched in their hands. "We didn't do it alone," she said. "Tumblebrook saved itself. We just... reminded it how."

"Well," Clara said, scratching behind Lady Grey's ears, "some of us gave more than reminders."

Lady Grey flicked her tail with dignified agreement.

The town council had voted unanimously to restore all original land boundaries. North Star Land Group had been dissolved. The developer's temporary office cleared. Monarch Society assets were now under federal audit. As for Vincent Pike—last spotted in Vermont, managing a llama sanctuary and allegedly refusing to speak to anyone who mentioned a garden permit.

With the truth aired and corruption cut at the root, the town felt lighter. Busier. Whole.

"I've been thinking," Amelia said, setting her glass down. "About reopening the old stables."

Clara blinked. "The one with the haunted loft and the weather vane that screams like a banshee during storms?"

"That's the one."

"What for?"

Amelia's smile was slow and sure. "Community space. Historical lectures. Murder mystery weekends, maybe."

Lady Grey sat upright and gave a small chirp—a sound that, if you listened closely, could be mistaken for approval.

Clara grinned. "That tracks. Around here, the mystery writes itself."

From below the porch, Mr. Lark passed with a crate of newly donated books for Gossamer Fables. Across the street, Doris waved a cinnamon roll triumphantly at Officer Wexley, who looked increasingly overwhelmed by a group of visiting garden club ladies peppering him with questions. Even Ezra had promised to unveil a new painting at the inn once the summer exhibit opened.

It wasn't just survival.

It was rebirth.

As the sun dipped lower, casting golden fingers across the lake, Amelia leaned into the railing beside Lady Grey. Her heart felt steady now—anchored. Tumblebrook was far from perfect, but it was home. And it was hers again.

Lady Grey's ears twitched.

From beyond the ridge came a faint rustle—not threatening, not urgent. Just... curious.

Another secret, perhaps. Another story waiting to be told.

Lady Grey slipped down from the railing and padded toward the edge of the porch.

"Already?" Clara asked, following her gaze.

Amelia smiled—the kind of smile worn by those who've learned that peace is not the absence of mystery, but the grace of living alongside it.

"Let her look," she said softly. "That's how it always begins."